BACK-UP GUN

Pepperdine was slammed against the door at his back so hard the knob gouged him. He was dazed for five seconds. One of the men farther back said, "Bust him in two, Jed, an' let's get back to the saloon."

Hugh's vision cleared as the bulky man set himself for a belly blow. He was starting to twist sideways to avoid the blow when his bad knee gave way and he started to stagger and fall.

The bulky man's rock-hard fist caught Hugh in the side as he was going down. From across the road a gravelly voice sang out, "Step back, you son of a bitch. Get away from him."

The four rangemen turned. Another older man was nearing the center of the road on his march from the gun shop. He was holding a short-barreled shotgun in his hands, both hammers hauled back.

"You deaf?" McGregor snarled. "I said get away from the door. Move back into the road. *Move!*" McGregor halted in the middle of the starlit road, both barrels of his scattergun aimed directly at the rigid range riders. . . .

Also by Lauran Paine:

ASSASSIN'S WORLD

BANNON'S LAW

DAKOTA DEATHTRAP

GERMAN MILITARY INTELLIGENCE IN WORLD
  WAR II: The Abwehr

THE MARSHALL

SKYE

TANNER

WITCHCRAFT & THE MYSTERIES: A Grimoire

THE HORSEMAN*

THE NEW MEXICO HERITAGE*

*Published by Fawcett Books

THE GUNS
OF SUMMER

Lauran Paine

FAWCETT GOLD MEDAL • NEW YORK

CHAPTER ONE

Springtime

The town of Sheridan grew out of the ash and rubble of an earlier settlement known as Hide Town, where buffalo hunters had stacked hides like cordwood to be freighted to a railroad siding sixty miles east. In those earlier days the settlement had three log structures: a saloon, a mercantile store, and a combination harness and gun works.

Hide Town suffered two Indian attacks. The first one was a sortie of combined tribesmen whom the buffalo hunters fought off without much difficulty. It resulted in a half-dozen deaths but little material damage.

The second attack was by three full-strength war parties who arrived before dawn and departed the following afternoon with Hide Town in flames, its ragtag population drastically reduced. When the Indians left as they had arrived, in a storm of dust and noise, most of Hide Town's horses went with them.

Hide Town never recovered. For seven years the only inhabitants of the place were a pair of brothers named

Farnsworth, who made a bare-bones living by trapping in winter and pot-hunting in summer.

The Farnsworths eventually disappeared. By the time Hide Town was buried beneath the new settlement, with a soldier-fort a mile and a half eastward, only once in a great while did anyone arrive who recalled the earlier place. The new settlement was named Sheridan after a Union general. New log buildings were erected, but along Main Street there were also structures of red brick.

Sheridan throve with the arrival of stockmen, a stage company corralyard and office, a cafe, and, much later, another red brick building that housed the Sheridan Bank & Trust Company.

By that time there were large trees on both sides of Main Street, a town council, a sluice that carried water into town, a town law officer, and a dozen business establishments.

No one had encountered Indians near Sheridan for a long while. But it was rumored there were hideouts in the mountains that curved horseshoe-fashion around the Sheridan plain to the north, east, and west.

There could indeed have been holdouts up in there somewhere; occasionally some stockmen whose animals strayed beyond the foothills mentioned finding stone rings, hide stretchers made of peeled poles, and blurry, soft tracks that could have been made by moccasins.

If there were redskins hiding out in the mountains, they were not troublesome. At least none of the annoying things that happened on the range or in town were blamed on them.

Hugh Pepperdine, who had the saddle and harness works in Sheridan, had once made a statement in Rusty Morton's saloon, The Drover's Home, that reflected the attitude of most people about Indians. Hugh had said, "I figure the tomahawks are more scairt of us than we are of them," implying that if there were hideouts, they were very careful to keep out of sight. Although the Indian wars had been over for quite a while, there were still young army officers in need of notoriety who would have liked nothing better than to lead a regiment against anyone in hide pants who was not on a reservation.

Sheridan had four main roadways leading into and out of town. With the founding of new towns farther south and west, freighting became an important source of Sheridan's revenue. So did ranching. The cattlemen came to fill the void left by the departed tribesmen. A few had come earlier and had lost men as well as cattle to war parties, but by the time Hank Dennis established his mercantile and general store, stockmen had free run of the entire Sheridan plain without reason to look over their shoulders.

Hank made money from the first time he opened his doors. He also began to put on a little blubber and to lose some hair. Right now the main focus of his civic concern was Sheridan's lack of respectability. Hank Dennis was a Southern Baptist. He went before the town council and offered to buy and donate land in the middle of town if the council would pony up half the cost of a church. He'd put up the other half.

The council seemed delighted with the idea, except for one man, Pete Donner, who had been born Pierre Donnier, had come to America in his mother's arms, and had barely survived after cholera carried off both parents in New York.

Pete was a suspicious man with dark hair and eyes and an olive complexion that burned Indian-brown during summertime. Pete wanted to know what kind of a church Hank Dennis had in mind. When Hank said a decent

Baptist church, Pete Donner simply nodded his head as though in confirmation of an earlier suspicion and voted against Hank's offer.

No church was built. Hank argued himself blue in the face. He even stated forthrightly in front of the entire town council that Pete Donner's vote against was only one vote and there were three other councilmen.

Pete Donner was president of the Sheridan Bank & Trust Company. The three other councilmen had loans at his bank. Hank did not; he owed nothing to anyone. He was probably the only merchant in Sheridan who was completely solvent. No church was built.

Hugh Pepperdine was a lanky, graying man with leathery skin, shrewd little pale eyes, a wide mouth, and work-callused hands. He had been an army scout, a mule skinner, and even once over in Idaho a peace officer, but, as he had confided in James McGregor, whose gunsmithing shop was two doors north of Morton's saloon, when a man gets into his forties he ought to get into a line of work with a roof overhead, shade in summer, and an iron stove in winter. Where Hugh had learned the saddle and harness maker's trade was anyone's guess, but he was very good at both.

McGregor, who was a head shorter than Hugh Pepperdine, with rusty-reddish hair, blue eyes, and a bullheaded set to his jaw, was about Pepperdine's age, somewhere very near or into his fifties. James McGregor was a widower. He was also a taciturn individual except with one or two men around town, including Hugh Pepperdine.

McGregor kept a speckled-ware coffeepot on his stove in the gunshop summer and winter. He and Hugh were generally in agreement on most things, but on one thing they absolutely disagreed—chewing tobacco. Hugh had chewed since he was just barely tall enough to rig out a horse. McGregor had tried tobacco once, had been deathly sick, and from that time on had detested the stuff.

He would not have admitted it if they'd dragged him behind wild horses, but he was in awe of his friend's ability to drink whiskey and chew tobacco at the same time. It should have made Hank as sick as a tanyard pup, but it never did.

McGregor's gunsmithing ability ran in the family, he often said. His father and grandfather had been gunsmiths in the Old Country. But gunsmithing by itself, even in a country where everyone owned at least one gun and just about everyone old enough to shave carried one, paid barely enough to maintain James McGregor's overhead. He was also an engraver and a silversmith, trades that augmented his income.

Like some methodical perfectionists, James McGregor's silver work had to please him in each detail or he'd melt it down and start over.

One time Hugh was watching James make a large silver concho for a cattleman's headstall. It had a rope-rolled, raised edge. James was working from the original concho of a pair, of which the cattleman had lost one. Hugh thought James's duplication was perfect. McGregor looked up dourly as he raised the completed concho to drop it back into the hot little steel pot to be remelted, and had said, "You won't sit still if you do something wrong on a saddle. Why should I be any different?"

Hugh had sipped his coffee, grinned, tongued his wad to the opposite cheek, and had murmured, "Pigheaded Scotchman."

McGregor's predictable reaction as he leaned to look into the melting pot was to say, "Pigheaded Yankee. I've seen you cuss blue over a piece of leather that didn't set right."

Pepperdine and McGregor were in Rusty Morton's saloon on the blustery, cold spring evening when the southbound stage rattled down Main Street as far as the palisaded corralyard. A half hour later, when the whip entered the saloon buttoned to the gullet, tugging off his gloves, they made room for him at the bar, a courtesy which he acknowledged with a nod and a smile. "Colder'n a witch's tit," he exclaimed before banging on the bartop for service.

He loosened his hip-length sheep-pelt-lined coat as he asked if the marshal was in town. Hugh didn't answer because he didn't know, but McGregor knew. "I think so, I saw him ride in from the south about suppertime. Was there a light over at the jailhouse?"

The whip, who was reaching for his glass of whiskey, said, "Didn't look." He tipped his head and swallowed once, slapped the glass back down, and nodded at Rusty for a refill.

He blew out a rattling breath and smiled. "Now, that's better. It ain't supposed to be so cold this time of year, is it?"

Hugh thought it was. "I've seen it colder in July than it is right now."

Rusty returned with the refilled glass. The whip leaned on the bar in the stove-warmed, musty room, and although he curled thick fingers around the jolt glass, he did not lift it.

"I been drivin' through this town five, six years an' never yet set foot inside that bank with the brick front."

He raised the glass, dropped its contents straight down as he had done before, then pushed the glass away and turned slightly to his right as the heat worked on him from inside and outside.

He looked Pepperdine and McGregor up and down before speaking again, "The Sheridan bank ever been robbed?"

McGregor's eyes narrowed. "No. Why?"

"Eighty miles north up over the line into Colorado a bunch of outlaws raided a bank in a place called Bluestem." The whip paused. "Forty miles north of Sheridan, up at San Luis, they raided another bank couple days back." He paused again. "I left San Luis at midnight last night. There's not a lot to do on this kind of a run, so I got to speculatin' that those men are raidin' banks as they travel south. Maybe they figure to raid banks all the way down to the Mex border an' cross over where the law dassn't chase them, carryin' all the money they can pack."

Hugh thought for a moment, then abruptly walked to the roadway door and looked over the top of it, grunted, and walked back. "There's a light in the jailhouse," he told the coach driver.

The whip, who was a burly, red-faced man with a perpetual squint, said, "Much obliged," put down another silver coin, and marched out of the saloon into the windy, cold, dark night.

McGregor was nursing a half-full whiskey glass. "That don't make a whole lot of sense," he told his companion. "If those bank robbers aren't green as grass, they'd figure out someone would get to Sheridan before they could."

Hugh was carving off a fresh wad when he spoke. "For a fact," he said in agreement. "But if he's right about them robbing banks as they go along, they wouldn't have to raid our bank. They could go east or west a fair distance. There are other towns with banks in them."

Rusty Morton came along behind the bar. He was a stocky man with brown hair carefully combed on both sides of a line down the middle of his head. He had several elegant brocaded vests that he wore even during the hottest summer days. His skin was pale, his body pudgy, his face singularly unlined although he had to be close to fifty. He'd left a wife back in Missouri eleven years earlier, and recently he'd heard that she had divorced him and remarried. He lived at the Sheridan Hotel, which was actually a rooming house at the north end of town, on the west side of Main Street.

He pulled up his sleeve garters and leaned on the bar as he said, "What did you say about a bank gettin' robbed?"

Hugh told him. He also explained the whip's theory that the robbers were making raids as they headed southward, maybe toward the Mexican border.

Rusty fixed the lanky Pepperdine with a steady stare. "Our bank, for crissake?"

James McGregor's face brightened sardonically. "Serves you right for havin' money there," he said. Rusty ignored McGregor. "Has anyone told the marshal?"

Hugh thought they had by now. "The whip went over there."

Rusty loosened a little. "Nobody's stupid enough to rob one bank after another, all in the same southward direction."

McGregor came right back. "They did it twice, Rusty.

Evidently they didn't get caught, or the whip wouldn't have come into town lookin' for Marshal Fogarty."

Morton said nothing for a while, not until someone up the bar rapped several times hard with a thick beer mug. Then, as he was straightening up, he said, "Is it a gang of 'em?"

Neither Hugh nor McGregor could answer that, so Morton had to depart without getting an answer. James watched him for a moment before speaking. "I guess now we know who's got a pile of money in Donner's bank, don't we?"

The harness maker nodded. "Yeah. An' I guess we know who don't have. You an' me."

A stray thought made McGregor broadly smile. "Pete Donner'll have a fit if they tell him. Ever since I've known him he's been worryin' about his bank gettin' robbed."

CHAPTER TWO

Saturday

No one seemed to have told Donner there were bank robbers in the territory because the following day, with a cold wind still blustering, he came down to the harness works to have his belt lengthened a little with new holes punched into it, and Hugh mentioned the stage driver from up north and what he had said.

Donner, who was not a smiling man, had small, very dark eyes and a bear-trap mouth. He leaned on the counter staring as Pepperdine took the belt to his sewing horse, sat down, and clamped the belt into place to remove the buckle and keeper before he made a splice that would not show.

"Bluestem and San Luis?" he exclaimed. "They're in a straight line from one another southward."

Hugh cut stitches holding the buckle and keeper in place. "Uh-huh," he agreed without looking up from his work. "That's what the whip said; looked to him like they was heading to Mexico, raidin' as they went."

Pete Donner did not take his eyes off Pepperdine as the lanky harness maker went to his worktable to skive leather and fit the splice before returning to the sewing horse.

"Bluestem's what—about forty, fifty miles above San Luis?" Donner said.

"Something like that," replied Hugh in an absentminded way as he picked up the awl and two harness needles to start the stitching.

"San Luis is forty miles north of Sheridan."

"Yep."

Donner's olive complexion paled slightly. He did not speak as he watched Pepperdine sew. The long silence made Hugh raise his eyes. "Like McGregor said, they don't have to raid down here, Pete. They could maybe do better raiding towns east or west of here."

Donner did not appear to be placated. When Hugh brought him the belt, he slapped down a silver coin, held in his stomach as he ran the belt through trouser loops, buckled it, and let his stomach out. The belt fit perfectly. He said, "Much obliged."

Pepperdine leaned forward over his counter. "I expect Joe Fogarty knows, Pete. That stage driver went over to see him last night."

The banker looked steadily at the taller and older man. "I'll go see him. I got less use for bank robbers than I got for anything on this earth."

Hugh smiled slightly and watched the banker leave the shop, heading southward in the direction of the marshal's office.

An hour later, as Hugh was at the sewing horse again, double-stitching a trace for the stage company up the road, Marshal Joe Fogarty walked in. He nearly hid the sunlight when he passed through the doorway. Joe was not just tall, he was also thick. He had coppery-colored hair, a turned-up nose, and eyes as blue as cornflowers.

He was well into his thirties, unmarried, and thoroughly capable.

Hugh paused at his work and pointed to the coffeepot atop his iron stove. Marshal Fogarty nodded, acknowledged the silent invitation, but leaned over the counter instead of drawing off a cup. "You did it again, didn't you?" he said. "What you got against Pete, always stirring him up? He came into my office sweatin' like a stud horse."

Hugh's expression showed almost cherubic innocence as he replied. "I thought he knew. That story was goin' around last night, and in this town a man can't pee through a knothole without everyone in town knowing about it an hour later."

"He hadn't heard," stated the larger man, and finally went to fill a cup with black coffee, which he brought back to the counter with him. He tasted the coffee, which was as bitter as original sin, pushed the cup away, and shook his head. "Rusty Morton got me out of bed this morning. Since then Hank Dennis and everyone who's got money at the bank has been after me like the devil after a crippled saint."

Pepperdine restated what had been said before. "They don't have to be heading for Sheridan. Hell, there's bigger towns with banks in them east and west of here."

Joe Fogarty considered the coffee cup. "When did you make that stuff, Hugh?"

"Monday."

"This is Saturday."

"I know. Well, every now an' then I'd pitch in another fistful of coffee and fill the pot with fresh water."

Marshal Fogarty studied the harness trace clamped between the curved jaws of the sewing horse. "I sent that skinny gaffer who works at the livery barn to scout the northward country. He used to be an army tracker. If those outlaws are comin' straight south from San Luis, they'll be in my territory by today. If they're not already in it."

Pepperdine offered a suggestion. "You might set some boys to the east and west of us, Joe. Then with any luck you'd know if they bypassed Sheridan."

Fogarty seemed to ignore this, but evidently he took it in, because as he was turning to depart he said, "Is that how you did it when you was a deputy over in Idaho?"

"Yes. It's a different kind of country over there. Lots of deep canyons and hills. Not like New Mexico, where a man can see a hell of a distance on a clear day. But I never had to hunt bank robbers. There wasn't no banks where I worked. Lots of horse thieves though, and other varmints."

Fogarty stood back from the counter to watch a morning stage proceed northward at a dead walk. There was a town ordinance against driving fast on Main Street. He said, "Pete wants to send the bank's money out of town until this mess passes. Maybe down to Albuquerque." Fogarty turned back from watching the roadway. "I told him the worst thing a man could do with outlaws of any kind in the area would be to load a stage with money and send it away."

Hugh was gnawing a corner off his cut plug and did not comment, so Joe Fogarty strolled back to the sun-brightened roadway, turned up his collar against the wind, and headed for the general store.

Other visitors came to the harness shop. Because it was Saturday, ranchers, riders, womenfolk, and youngsters from the countryside were in town.

Hugh managed to get one trace completed, but there were too many interruptions during the afternoon for him to complete the other one. When the yard boss for the stage company came by for the tugs, Hugh waved toward the unfinished one and the yard boss left, heading across to The Drover's Home, which was the second most patronized business establishment in town on Saturday. The first was the general store.

By late afternoon, when most of the stockmen who had brought their families to town had loaded their rigs at the mercantile and headed for home, what remained was a lot of unattached rangemen. Joe Fogarty was very visible; there were fights almost every Saturday. This time there were none.

Hugh Pepperdine got rid of his last customer with the sun red and low in the west, locked up, and crossed diagonally toward McGregor's gunshop.

Like just about every other business establishment in Sheridan, the gunshop had had its share of visitors, of which a few were even customers. When Hugh walked in, James was completing the sale of a reblued and newly stocked six-gun to a swarthy man with a neatly trimmed black beard.

Hugh headed for the coffeepot and remained in the background as he sipped. McGregor was busy right up until shadows were lengthening and broadening. Then, with his last customer gone, he removed a greasy apron, ran both hands down his trousers, and in silence drew off his own cup of coffee. His eyes met Hugh's as he raised his cup. "Do any business today?" he asked.

Pepperdine nodded. "A little. You?"

"A little. That feller with the black beard was the best. Fifteen dollars for that gun. I bought it off a broke cowboy for two and fixed it up. I hope it shoots straight."

McGregor lowered his cup, gazing through a dirty

window into the roadway. Opposite his store was the red-brick bank building. "Pete's been ducking in and out of there like a cat on a hot tin roof."

Pepperdine accepted this without looking across the road. "Joe's worried too. He'll make a show like he isn't, but he's sweating."

McGregor leaned to refill his cup. "He's not the only one. Rusty and Hank Dennis been over to the bank a couple of times that I saw, an' maybe more."

"Withdrawing their money, you reckon?"

James raised gray eyes to his friend's face. "I sort of had that idea. Hide it under the bed, maybe, or in a coffee can in the outhouse. That driver sure stirred up a hornet's nest, didn't he?"

Hugh turned slightly to watch the roadway with its restless movement and shadows. "I wonder who those outlaws are. Must be a gang of them." Hugh considered the grounds at the bottom of his cup. "That'd be a hell of a way to make a living."

McGregor agreed. "For a fact. I just barely get by, but at least when I go to bed at night I don't have to worry about some lawman kickin' in the door and pointin' a gun at my head."

"Or shootin' the horse out from under you. Or aimin' for your back as you race out of town."

McGregor put his empty cup into a bucket of oily water on the floor behind the stove where the coffeepot simmered. "That feller with the whiskers who bought the gun today—he's a preacher."

Hugh was interested. "Did he tell you that?"

"Yeah. He had passed out flyers around town. He's holdin' a camp meetin' east of town in the cottonwood grove tomorrow. He left one of the flyers. Want to see it?"

"Not especially," the harness maker replied dryly.

"You might want to go, Hugh."

Pepperdine eyed his friend coolly. "If you mean my soul needs saving, I might say the same about yours."

"Not that. The flyer asks that the womenfolk bring food out there. They'll do it too. Camp meetings on Sunday are real celebrations. A man can get full as a tick for no more'n the two bits he puts in when the preacher passes the hat."

"Are you going, James?"

"There's nothing else to do tomorrow, and the food will be plentiful. About the preaching, it don't affect me one way or another. Want to come along?"

"I've got a trace to finish for the stage company, and I thought since I couldn't get it done today and they're in a big hurry for it, maybe I'd keep the roadway door locked tomorrow and get caught up a little."

McGregor accepted that. After his friend had departed, he went down to the tonsorial parlor, paid his two bits for the use of the bathhouse, got a threadbare towel and a chunk of tan soap, and went out back to pump water. The short path between the pump and the bathhouse was slippery from water being sloshed by other men carrying buckets back and forth, as it was every Saturday night.

The town sounds did not so much abate after sundown as they became different. Rusty Morton was as busy as a kitten in a box of shavings. This, too, occurred every Saturday night. He had once told Joe Fogarty that if it weren't for Saturday nights, the saloon business in a place like Sheridan wouldn't pay a man for the expense of keeping a saloon stocked.

Joe hadn't believed him. It had been his experience that people who said things like that were making money.

The ones who really were not making money looked like they weren't, and Rusty Morton's elegant brocaded vests, of which he had about a dozen and wore a different one every day, cost a lot of money.

Joe was taking time off from intimidating rangemen with his size and reputation as an individual capable of handling any kind of trouble by having a late supper at the cafe when McGregor walked in smelling of lilacs.

Marshal Fogarty recognized the scent; it was the only kind used at the tonsorial parlor, and he also knew what McGregor had done—taken a bath because it was Saturday night.

They grunted a little back and forth before the marshal paid up and abandoned his seat at the counter. The seat was immediately taken by a burly, black-bearded man with a dusty hat and a pleasant smile.

McGregor smiled back. He could afford to. Some of the fifteen dollars this stranger had paid for the gun was what James would use to pay for his supper.

CHAPTER THREE

The Camp Meeting

McGregor was right. The womenfolk were up late Saturday night and early Sunday morning organizing hampers of food for the camp meeting. Their husbands, fathers, and brothers, who had not gotten to bed until past midnight, were dragooned into hitching up and loading buggies and wagons to transport food and families a mile northeast to the cottonwood grove that had been the site of camp meetings over the years when itinerant preachers had passed through.

This happened irregularly and infrequently. The men might not have missed it, but the womenfolk, all of whom saw it as their duty to bring up children as practicing Christians, favored these meetings. They turned them into hymn-singing celebrations complete with happy fraternizing accompanied by mounds of food and blessings for the Lord on His day.

From behind the closed front of his shop Hugh Pepperdine watched the exodus with mixed feelings. He was not a family man and it had troubled him now and then that he was not. Because he was liked in the community, Hugh was included in most civic events, unless they were for families only.

He went behind the counter to stitch the harness tug before the last wagon and buggy left town. He did not see James McGregor in his unironed but clean white shirt hitch a ride to the cottonwood grove with Hank Dennis. McGregor was shaved, his boots had been stove-blacked, and his britches were clean. Whether he felt the enthusiasm of those around him on the drive out and at the camp-meeting site or not, his appearance suggested that he did.

Someone had set up trestle tables. Tree shade would keep the place cool. Women officiously bustled here and there. The preacher, bible under one arm, his hat brushed clean and his suit of rusty black appropriate to the occasion, mingled well, pumped hands, laughed with the children, and helped with the food until his practiced eye told him the crowd was large enough for services to begin.

Pepperdine stitched in a town that had become unnaturally quiet, although most Sundays were more restrained than weekdays.

Harness traces were usually four thicknesses of leather, two of which were doubled. They were of back leather, never shoulder, neck, or belly. They were used as the crucial parts of a hauling harness, which made them difficult to mend.

Hugh made his awl hole first, pulled through one needle with waved and twisted flax thread, then the other needle similarly equipped. He pulled each stitch tight, let the needles hang while he picked up the awl to make the next hole, and repeated the procedure. It was tedious work. An experienced harness maker could sew one trace in less than a day, excluding interruptions. Not all harness makers were pleased to have someone bring in tugs to be mended.

Hugh wasn't. In city shops they usually had apprentices, young people who wanted to learn the trade, to sew tugs. Hugh had encountered few people that interested in the saddler's and harness maker's profession, and none at all in Sheridan.

It did not help his vague feeling of exclusion when the muted, faint sound of people singing hymns came down into the empty and silent town to him.

Once when he glanced up he saw that thin, older hostler from the livery barn Marshal Fogarty had sent out to scout up the countryside yesterday stroll past. He went to the saloon, found the doors locked, rattled them annoyedly for a moment, then shuffled southward as far as the mercantile building, where he sat down on a bench bolted to the front wall, shoved out thin legs, and slumped.

Hugh did not remember the hostler's name, but he remembered rumors about the man's drinking habits. He went back to his sewing; it seemed that most hostlers drank. At least the ones Hugh had known had been drinking men. Of course, this was not exclusive to corralyard men and livery barn hostlers, but they seemed to do it a little more than most folks.

He finished one side, unslung the jaws of his sewing horse, turned the tug over, reset the jaws, and made his first awl hole, leaving the awl in the leather while he rethreaded both needles, rolled the flax thread on his upper leg until the strands were tight, then drew them slowly through a ball of wax. He did this twice before straddling the horse to thread the needles.

Now he removed the awl and started sewing. He made one stitch, paused to glance down where the hostler had

been sitting, and watched, awl in hand, as a range rider
swung off at the tierack in front of the store, looped his
reins, and smiled as he called a greeting to the hostler.

The rangeman stepped around to the bench and sat
down, removed his hat to beat dust from it against his
leg, then carelessly dumped the hat back atop his head.
Hugh could not hear the man speak, but he saw the
hostler reply. The stranger smilingly looked up through
town as he got comfortable on the bench. He and the
hostler seemed to enjoy each other's company.

The rangeman was a stranger to Hugh Pepperdine, but
this time of year, with the ranches hiring and firing, with
riders coming into town looking for work and sometimes
passing on through, Hugh saw about as many men in
town that he did not know as those he did know.

He went back to his sewing. An hour later, with the
hymn-singing drifting mutedly to him, he went to the
stove for a cup of java.

The hostler and rangeman were still on the bench in
front of Dennis's store, relaxed in their desultory
conversation. Hugh stood by the stove sipping coffee for
a while, his interest in the two men upon the far side of
the road southward dwindling to indifference.

Joe Fogarty had been right. For a fact, the coffee was
bitter. He would make a fresh batch tomorrow, Monday,
which was when he ordinarily emptied out the grounds
and put in fresh ones with clean water anyway.

A rat-tailed dog went southward at the edge of the
plankwalk on Hugh's side of the roadway, sniffing for
scraps someone might have thrown out. He found a piece
of chewed jerky in front of the harness shop and stopped
long enough to swallow it before resuming his southward
foraging.

Hugh sighed, straddled the horse, and went back to

work. Faint hymn-singing reached him again. It was customary for camp meetings to use up an entire Sunday morning, and if the food held out, they could go right on into the afternoon.

Hugh paused to grope for his cut plug, bit off a ragged corner, and got back to work. He was reaching for the trace when he felt his building quiver. Simultaneously with this startling occurrence he heard a muffled sound as though someone had fired a cannon in the distance.

He stopped short as reverberations made waves of soundless disturbance that rattled the coffee cup he'd placed on a shelf near the stove. Calipers, harness hardware, and tin patterns hanging on the walls also rattled.

He sat motionless, too startled to think rationally. Once in Arizona many years back he'd experienced an earthquake. This diminishing sensation was identical to that event.

He leaned to look across the roadway southward. The livery barn hostler was sitting straight up. The man beside him had reset his hat. He said something to the hostler and arose to approach his horse. The skinny man suddenly sprang up from the bench. He flung up a bony arm to point with and said something that brought the range rider to a halt. He turned and walked back to the hostler without haste, and while the skinny older man was staring northward, the stranger hit him across the top of the head with a gun barrel, stepped over the body, unlooped his reins, turned the horse, swung across leather, and passed from Hugh's sight toward the lower end of town. He had done none of these things in haste.

Hugh always had trouble with the lock of his roadway door. He had it now. By the time he got the door yanked open, there was no sign of the rangeman. Nor of the rat-tailed dog. He stepped outside and was immediately struck by a strong acrid scent. He'd blown enough boulders and stumps to recognize it at once. Dynamite!

He whirled around facing northward in the direction of the Sheridan Bank & Trust Company's brick building. The steel shutters were in place in front of the glass windows. Around them a faint but discernible sifting of dust was moving outward.

Hugh let go a sizzling curse, darted back into his shop for the belt and gun hanging from a peg on the back wall, and hurried back toward the roadway. As he buckled the belt into place, he heard running horses somewhere behind town on the west side.

He ran unheedingly through an overgrown lot between his building and the abstract company's building south-ward, stumbled over a discarded buggy tire before he reached the alley, and stopped in a cloud of dust that was still rising.

The men on horseback were near the lower end of town, bunched up because the alley had buildings on both sides, when Hugh stepped to the center of the alley and raised his six-gun to cock it. The distance was a little far for a handgun, but with those riders pushed close together before they got clear of town, where they could fan out, a bullet was almost certainly going to hit flesh of some kind, human or horse.

Someone yelled behind him. Hugh dropped flat in the dirt, his gun discharging on impact. The bullet went skyward, and a horseman ran over him, careening after the other men farther down the alley.

The rider was balancing a cocked six-gun in his right fist. He looked back through swirling dust to where Hugh was fighting against a fiercely spiraling pain in his lower body as he tried to raise himself up enough to get off a shot.

The horseman fired first, missed by a yard as his horse hurtled ahead in a belly-down run, and cocked his weapon for the second shot. Hugh got off a shot, and knew it had gone wide as he was recovering from the recoil.

The fleeing man's second shot struck wood somewhere behind the harness maker, then the outlaw faced forward and rode low as he raced away.

Hugh did not fire again. He dropped the weapon and rolled up into a sitting position to examine the bloody tear in his right trouser where the calked shoe of a thousand-pound horse had come down on his leg, not on the kneecap but to one side of it, pinching flesh and cloth and badly tearing both.

Hugh Pepperdine had experienced pain many times, but this was the worst. It made him sick to his stomach. He dug for his clasp knife, slit the trouser leg to see his injury better, then sat there a moment breathing deeply as pain washed through him in waves.

It was not a fatal wound. It was not even a very serious one, but he doubted that a bullet through the body could have caused as much pain.

For a while he simply sat there in the dust and dirt, then eventually pushed himself up to his feet. He looked around for something to lean on, then closed his eyes for a moment, gritted his teeth, and started hobbling toward the back door of his shop, dripping blood in a steady stream as he progressed out of the alleyway.

His gun was still lying out there.

He was conscious of nothing but his injury after he got inside, where there was a bucket of fresh drinking water and some clean rags. He bound the injury to stop the bleeding, but had to loosen the cloth as the wound began to swell. He sat on an old chair with a rawhide bottom and an uneven balance, holding the painful leg out. He had a bottle of popskull behind the counter, but it might as well have been on the moon. Hobbling inside from the alley had used up about all the willpower he possessed. He didn't even feel like digging out his cut plug.

It gradually seemed to him that the silence throughout town was as it had been an hour earlier. Then the hymn-singing began again and he swore through clenched teeth. That coach driver had been right; they *were* raiding southward.

They had just blown the safe of Pete Donner's bank, muffling the explosion some way, and were riding hell-for-leather away from town, probably with every dime that had been in the damned safe.

He could have shot one, maybe more than one of them, if he'd looked behind instead of in front when he ran into the alley. What the hell was that last one doing behind him anyway?

Finally, after a quarter of an hour, he stood on one foot, leaned forward as far as possible to get both hands on the countertop, and hopped. Using the countertop, he got around behind into his working area and found his whiskey bottle.

The wound was not as painful now, probably because his leg was getting numb, but there was a strong aching sensation. He took down two swallows, set the bottle atop the counter, and looked around to see how close he was to his cutting table. He was close enough to hitch up one hip and get into a perched position on the table with all weight off both legs. The pain returned as he gained this position. He took two more swallows from the bottle. The pain was probably still down there, but he was less aware of it.

That rangeman who had been sitting on the bench across the road, the one who had brained the hostler, sure as hell had been their lookout. Recalling how the stranger had stepped back to knock the hostler unconscious, without haste, without any indication of nervousness, and had then strolled to his horse, climbed up, and trotted toward the lower end of town convinced Pepperdine that he had been ridden down by another member of a very professional band of outlaws.

He reached again for the bottle.

CHAPTER FOUR

Turmoil

The uproar lasted far into the night, with agitated people crowding into the harness shop to ask the same questions over and over, until Hugh locked his front door and took the lamp into the lean-to built onto the rear of the building that served as his living quarters.

He removed his boots, set the lamp on a table, and sat on the edge of the bunk to remove his blood-stiff britches so he could rebandage his wound. The entire knee area was not just badly swollen, it was also purple with a sickly tan border around the discoloration. It was as sore as a boil.

His third bandaging attempt was no more professional than the others had been, but this time it was much looser.

He was leaning back on the bed when someone rapped on the lean-to door and said, "McGregor. Open up."

It required effort accompanied by profanity to get from the bed to the south wall, but he made it, opened the door, did not greet the gunsmith but turned to slide a chair ahead as a crutch until he got back to the edge of the bed, where he pushed the chair aside and eased down very carefully.

McGregor studied his friend's face first, then the injured leg. He said, "Did you see him when he shot you?"

"No, I didn't see the son of a bitch. Not very well, anyway, because of the dust, an' he didn't shoot me, he rode his horse right over the top of me. Sit down, James. Hand me that whiskey bottle, will you?"

McGregor passed over the bottle and eased down on the nearby chair. "I had a feeling I should stay in town this morning."

Pepperdine leaned to place the bottle on the floor as he said, "I don't know that it would have helped. Have you talked to the marshal or Pete Donner?"

"Yes. The marshal was out at the prayer meeting with everyone else."

"They cleaned out the bank?"

"Right down to the silver in the clerk's box. Six thousand dollars in round figures."

Hugh touched his swollen knee very gently. McGregor leaned a little closer to look at it as he said, "Is it broken?"

"No. The horse's shoe had heel calks. It glanced off my kneecap and squeezed the hide to the inside and tore it. I never felt anything that hurt as much in my damned life, but it's nothing a man can't walk away from. In time. Look at the size of the thing. Big as a pumpkin . . . . Six thousand dollars?"

"And the silver. There are a lot of pretty darned upset folks in town. When the ranchers hear about it, they'll be stormin' into town to raise a ruckus too."

"I told Joe Fogarty about a stranger who rode in and

sat on a bench across the road with that skinny hostler,"
Hugh said.

"I heard about that. The hostler must've had an
eggshell skull. He's deader'n a rock. Did you get a good
look at that stranger?"

Hugh nodded. These were pretty much the same
questions he had been answering all afternoon and into
the late evening. "Yeah. That one I saw pretty good."
Hugh straightened up from touching his knee. "Is that
preacher still around?"

McGregor shrugged. "Darned if I know. Why, you
want to see him?"

"James, until you prayin' folks got back to town, I
had plenty of time to think. First off, tell me something:
Did you ever sell a handgun to a preacher before?"

"Not that I recollect, Hugh."

"Well, like I just said, I did some thinking. First off,
there was this band of renegades that raided up at
Bluestem. Then, ridin' south, they raided the bank at
San Luis. Then they come down here and raided us. An'
I haven't heard any of them was caught."

"All right. Go on."

"I watched one of them today. The feller who killed
the skinny feller. He was as calm as a toad, even after he
hit the hostler over the head. He walked over, turned his
horse, and mounted up as calm as anything. James, him
and those others was real professionals at their trade. Tell
me how it happens that a preacher rode in yesterday, got
a big prayer meetin' organized so's everyone would be
out of town . . ."

McGregor eased back slowly on the unsteady chair,
gazing steadily at his friend. He did not make a sound.

"And there's something else. When they blew the safe
I was right here in the shop an' the only sound I heard

was like someone maybe firing a cannon a couple of miles away. How did they manage that?"

McGregor had the answer. "They piled five mattresses in front of the door with the charge behind it. You ought to see the inside of the bank. There's mattress stuffin' everywhere, even on the ceiling and in the cracks in the walls like it was drove in with a chisel an' a hammer."

Hugh regarded his friend solemnly. "Mattresses? You mean they come into town packin' mattresses?"

McGregor could not answer that. "All I know is that's how they múffled the blast. And it sure worked; nobody out at the camp meetin' heard a thing. I sure didn't." McGregor tipped the chair back. "The preacher?"

"He come along and got everyone out of town."

McGregor rocked back and forth as he thought this over. Finally he said, "I got to tell you, Hugh, that when he wanted to buy a handgun and told me was a preacher, I was downright puzzled. Not that he didn't have every right. A man's got to defend himself no matter what his callin' is, but I don't recall ever having seen a minister wearing sidearms before."

Hugh scowled. "Did you tell this to Joe?"

"No. What did you tell him?"

"I only told him what I saw and what happened. I never got a chance to tell him what I thought because after we talked he ran out of the shop and everyone else came in. I had folks come in who haven't been in the shop in a couple of years. My leg was hurting something fierce, so after a while I cleared 'em out and locked up."

"Joe ought to hear more from you," stated McGregor. "He's going around town like a chicken with its head cut off. There are more stories going around than you could make up in a lifetime." McGregor arose. "Could I fetch Joe over here tonight?"

Pepperdine grimaced. He was sore and tired, his leg hurt, and his insides felt like they'd been varnished with whiskey. "In the morning, James. I'm worn to a frazzle and my leg's giving me hell."

"If you want to ride the stage down to Bordenton where they got a doctor, I'll make the arrangements and we could leave first thing in the morning."

"Naw. It hurts, but it's nothing to go that far about. It'll feel better in a day or two."

After McGregor had departed, the harness maker lay back to rest and fell asleep. He awakened in the middle of the night to hear a rat gnawing on wood outside his lean-to. The rat bothered him a lot less than the waste of coal oil, because the lamp was still burning. When he eased over to stand up, his injured leg was as stiff as a ramrod, but there was not much pain, so he hitched over to blow down the lamp mantle and hitched back in darkness to the bed, where he undressed and crawled under the quilts. Within moments he was asleep again.

The next time he awakened someone was banging on the lean-to door. He rubbed his eyes, sat up, called out to whoever it was to come back in an hour, and did not leave the bed for another fifteen minutes.

His injury had undergone some sort of metamorphosis during the night. The pain was localized in the immediate area of the wound itself, with very little elsewhere in the knee joint.

He made this discovery when he arose to pull on his britches and go to the washrack out back to shave and scrub, comb his hair, and try to eradicate the taste of sour whiskey by using Dr. West's tooth powder on a soggy brush. For an hour afterward his mouth tasted of mint, which was a pleasant change.

He was also hungry, which he hadn't been last night. It was probably a good sign that this morning he had an appetite.

He limped very noticeably even after changing the bandage and cleaning the injury, but the pain was nowhere near as unbearable as it had been the previous night, which pleased him as he went out to the shop to unlock the roadway door.

Sunlight was bouncing off the most distant mountaintops to the west, and a little of it brushed shadows off the roofs on Hugh's side of town. Otherwise, Sheridan was still in shadow.

He went down to the cafe, using a crooked stick as a cane. He was the first customer of the day, for which he was grateful, and because the cafeman was never talkative, they exchanged little more than grunts as Hugh ate his first meal in ages.

He had paid up and was departing when the normal breakfast customers began arriving. They were for the most part single men such as the blacksmith's helper, a clerk from Dennis's store, and a couple of unshorn, unwashed hostlers from the stage company corralyard. None of them knew Hugh well enough to delay his departure.

He was behind his counter at the harness maker's shop considering the tug he had not completed yesterday, when Marshal Fogarty entered. They exchanged a greeting, got comfortable, and Hugh told Joe Fogarty everything he had told McGregor last night, and as much more as had come to him since. It required almost a full hour. Twice Joe Fogarty chased off customers, one of whom was the corralyard boss after his harness tugs.

Fogarty rolled and lit a quirley, eyed Hugh during a short period of silence, then said, "If you're right about that preacher, everyone in town could identify him. An' you can identify the feller who killed the hostler. But right now I got a posse ready to ride, been ready for an hour, so we better talk some more tonight when I get back. Unless there's something else. Maybe you've got an idea how many were in the gang and maybe the color of horses they was astride."

Hugh had to think back. His best recollection of the number of outlaws, including the one who had run him down, was seven or eight men. About their horses he remembered only that the horse that had run over him was a bay. The world was full of bay horses. Every other horse a man saw was a bay.

After Fogarty departed, Hugh eased very carefully astride the sewing horse, kept most of his weight off the injured leg, and resumed stitching the harness tug. He anticipated interruptions and he got them. Mostly, they were curious people. He was patient with them, answering questions without looking up from his work. When Hank Dennis came in about midday, his storekeeper's cloth apron rolled up and hooked under his belt, Hugh kept right on stitching as he said, "Howdy, Hank."

The storekeeper was an energetic, high-strung man in his fifties, lean, quick-eyed, and terse. He asked pretty much the same questions right up until he said, "Hugh, you deal with rangemen all the time. Do you recollect a shoulder brand made to look like a Chihuahua spur?"

Pepperdine stopped sewing and leaned on the jaws of his sewing horse. "Don't recall it, Hank. Don't recall it at all. There's a spur outfit up in central Colorado, and I expect other places."

Dennis shook his head in quick back-and-forth motions. "A *Chihuahua* spur, Hugh. You've seen them."

Pepperdine nodded. "Yeah. Most of my life. A coarse, rounded shank and a rowel as big as your palm. What about it?"

"That feller who killed the livery barn man was riding a bay horse with a Chihuahua spur brand on his left shoulder."

"How do you know that?"

"A freighter who hauls goods to me was comin' toward town yesterday afternoon and passed a man riding a bay horse with a Mex spur brand on his left shoulder. They exchanged waves and the rider kept right on loping southward."

Hugh continued to lean forward on the sewing horse. He said, "Hank, there's a million bay horses in the country. There may be some with a Mex shoulder brand. That's all that proves. You can fetch your freighter over here if you want. I'd like to hear him describe the rider. I saw him, too, for a couple of hours off an' on. I'd know that man anywhere. Fetch him over."

The storekeeper fidgeted. "I can't. I asked him to stay in town until Marshal Fogarty got back, but he had six or seven more stops to make west of Sheridan and wouldn't waste the time."

Hugh leaned back very slowly, then made a hopeless gesture with both arms and looked around for his dangling needles. "What your freighter saw, Hank, was a man riding south on a bay horse with a Mex brand. Tell Joe when he gets back to town."

Dennis fidgeted some more, watched Pepperdine resume his sewing, made a little snorting sound, and hastened out of the harness works. He crossed the roadway on a diagonal course and hurried back into his store.

Pepperdine was almost finished with the trace when

Pete Donner walked in out of the sunshine. That little blustery wind that had been blowing for several days was gone, and in its place was something close to summer heat. Donner was sweating and hatless. He mopped his forehead at the counter, then leaned, looking across where Pepperdine was making his back stitches preparatory to cutting the thread and finishing the job.

Donner waited, watching each move, his dark eyes as quick as a snake's. As Hugh was freeing his needles from the residue of waxed thread, the banker said, "Hugh, I'm putting up reward money. Two hundred dollars."

Pepperdine arose gingerly and hitched around to fling the completed tug beside its mate on the worktable before speaking. "Maybe that'll help," he said, "but it wouldn't interest me a whole lot, Pete. Not even if I could set a horse."

"Somebody had to see them running from town yesterday."

"Yeah. Hank had a freighter over there a while back who claimed he saw one of them."

"Where is he now?"

"Go ask Hank. I sure don't know."

The banker hurried from the store and Hugh leaned in the window to watch his beeline course stir roadway dust in the direction of the general store. When Pete Donner disappeared inside, Hugh went after his hat and walking stick. He was hungry again and maybe his luck would hold; maybe if he ate early again he could avoid more silly darned questions.

CHAPTER FIVE

Fogarty's Surprise

Marshal Fogarty returned with six men riding tired animals. The liveryman sweated and bitterly complained because now he had to do all the work himself. He was not by nature a man who enjoyed physical exertion. Having a paunch that hung over his belt probably contributed to his breathlessness.

Joe Fogarty disbanded his posse and headed for his jailhouse office. The town was fairly quiet. It was suppertime for one thing; for another, people could not maintain a mood of outrage indefinitely.

Fogarty laboriously wrote a letter by failing daylight, trudged over to drop it in the outside slot at the general store, then went up to the cafe.

He did not expect to be left in peace as he ate, and he wasn't. The cafeman's counter was about half full. And Lady Luck, whom Joe Fogarty had come to view with skepticism over the years, did it to him again. The vacant place beside him at the counter was taken by Hank Dennis, whose agitation over his lost savings had not diminished.

He ignored the way Marshal Fogarty was shoveling in food like a man who had not eaten all day, leaned over, and said, "Well? You get any sign of them?"

Joe chewed, reached for his coffee cup, washed the mouthful down, and turned slowly before replying. "No," he said, and went back to his meal.

The storekeeper was too engrossed with his own troubles to recognize the signs of annoyance. "Did you find their tracks? They sure as hell left tracks, Joe."

Fogarty continued to chew for a long time. "Yeah, they left tracks. Somebody did, anyway, but this is a busy time of year and those gents didn't stray off the road, so what we found was most likely their sign mixed in with all kinds of other signs, Hank."

The cafeman came to stand in silence, gazing at the storekeeper. Dennis said, "Coffee an' maybe stew if you got it," and turned immediately back toward the big peace officer. He mentioned the freighter who had met a man riding a bay horse with a spur brand, and Fogarty listened, chewed, swallowed, and asked the same question the harness maker had asked. "Where is he? I'd like to talk to him."

Dennis reddened. "He wouldn't lay over, Joe. He's somewhere to the west of Sheridan."

The marshal arose, dumped a scattering of silver beside his empty place, nodded to the cafeman, and walked out of the cafe.

Across the road in the encroaching dusk there was a glow of soft lamplight in the harness shop window. He could make out two men in there and held back just long enough to roll and light a smoke before starting across.

Hugh and James McGregor glanced up as the large man entered. Fogarty was dusty and looked drawn. Hugh pointed to the pot atop the wood stove, but Fogarty shook his head. Hugh misinterpreted this. "Fresh pot, made with the pot clean and all."

"Had enough at the cafe," replied the lawman, looking around for something to sit on. There were two old chairs held together by twisted wire. Fogarty went over to lean on the counter the way McGregor was doing. Hugh asked if Hank Dennis had told him about the freighter, and Joe nodded glumly. "Yeah." He paused to drop his smoke into a dented old brass spittoon half-full of very dark water. When he straightened up he said, "If I go chasin' after the freighter to the west, those raiders will be riding south."

The older men nodded about that without speaking. Before the lawman's arrival they had been discussing what Fogarty's statement implied: The outlaws were putting miles behind them while folks in Sheridan, including the lawman, were wasting time. But that was not all they had been discussing.

McGregor made a dry comment. "It'd be nice if we had a telegraph in town, wouldn't it?"

Fogarty gazed at the grizzled, shorter man pensively, then turned his attention back to the harness maker. "You didn't get a good look at the feller who rode you down?"

"Sure didn't."

"How about the one over in front of the store that busted the hostler's skull?"

"Saw him as plain as I see you right now," Hugh stated. "I'll remember his face as long as I live." When he finished his statement he eased his sore leg a little where he was straddling the sewing horse. "James an' I been talkin' about something else, Joe. They're riding fast. They didn't get caught up at Bluestem nor at San

Luis. They had a head start yesterday morning an' last night they—"

"Last night," the marshal interrupted to say, "they made a dry camp about twenty or so miles south. That's as far as I went with the posse before we turned back."

McGregor had a question. "Straight south?"

Fogarty nodded, shifted position on the counter, and said, "Straight south. Within three days they can be down at the Mex border. If I'd been able, I'd have stayed after them, but we rode our horses pretty hard. They wouldn't have held up much longer."

Hugh nodded. "Yeah. Now what?"

"Strike out first thing in the morning, favor the animals, and maybe get fresh ones from cow outfits as we keep after them." A long silence followed Fogarty's statement, so he looked from one man to the other and became defensive. "I don't have wings."

Hugh and James exchanged a look. McGregor said, "It was twenty miles before they made camp. That was last night. Bordenton's another twenty miles ahead, due south the way those sons of bitches been riding since they commenced raiding up in Colorado."

Fogarty, whose saddle weariness made him irritable, scowled at the gunsmith. "You already said it, James. We don't have no telegraph, so we can't warn Bordenton."

McGregor shuffled to the stove to fill a cup with black coffee. While he was doing this, Hugh Pepperdine fished among his pockets for the cut plug and worried off a cud, which he tongued into his cheek. He watched his friend return to the counter and put the cup aside. Hugh imperceptibly nodded, and the gunsmith said, "Joe, you go on up to the rooming house and get your sleep. Me'n

Hugh got a notion of how we can get pretty close to those raiders."

Fogarty eyed the gunsmith skeptically and spoke sarcastically. "You're goin' to sprout wings."

McGregor ignored that. "We're goin' out on the night coach for Bordenton. Maybe those gents will lie over in camp tonight and raid the Bordenton bank in the morning. The stage changes horses at the way station halfway along, then strikes out again. It travels all night. The way we got it figured, with some luck we should arrive in Bordenton tomorrow morning. If our luck don't hold, the gang will already have raided the bank and be headin' for the border again. If they are, the thievin' sons of bitches, we're going to take the next stage south and this time, barrin' breakdowns, we ought to maybe be able to get ahead of them."

Fogarty straightened, went to work methodically rolling a smoke, lighted it atop the lamp mantle, inhaled, exhaled, and was examining the burning end when he finally spoke. "My guess is that there are seven or eight of them." He waited for this intimidating statistic to have an effect. It did, but not as Joe expected. Hugh Pepperdine smiled while slowly working his jaws. "Well now, we got shotguns, handguns, and we'll take along a couple of rifles from the gunshop."

Fogarty started to speak, but McGregor spoke first. "Joe, if we can get ahead of them and get time to set up a bushwhack, the way we figure it, surprising them might make a hell of a lot of difference."

The marshal trickled smoke while staring at the worktable, where a tin pattern lay atop an unrolled cowhide. He quietly said, "You're crazy. Neither one of you will ever see fifty again. You're not gunslingers. You're not lawmen. After they raid Bordenton there'll be riders all over the territory like hornets. Two strangers armed to the gills . . .''

Hugh limped into position of a spittoon and let fly. He limped back and straddled the sewing horse again. "You're most likely right," he told the big lawman. "An' there's somethin' else: Didn't neither of us have a red cent in Pete's bank. But Pete's sittin' up there wringin' hands and waitin' for you to pull off a miracle, and Hank Dennis is tellin' everyone who enters the store if you don't do your duty an' get his savings back, he's goin' to the town council to get you fired. . . . Joe, all we're tryin' to do is set things to rights. I personally got less use for outlaws of any kind than I got for snakes. . . . You could sleep on the stage.''

Fogarty dropped ash, staring steadily at the harness maker and killed the smoke, raised a hand to reset his hat, and groaned. The silence lasted until someone across the road at the saloon barged out in the direction of the hitchrack singing at the top of his voice. Moments later the singing stopped, and the sound of a galloping horse leaving Sheridan by the north road took its place, diminishing as the rangeman continued on his way.

Fogarty finally spoke. "The night southbound stage is already gone. Look at that clock behind you.''

Pepperdine didn't look around. "No, it isn't. It's being held back.''

Fogarty's eyes narrowed as realization came. "Is that a fact? How did you get 'em to do that?''

"There's nothing goin' south but some light freight, so there don't have to be a tight schedule. An' Mr. Donner agreed to pay for the coach. Go ask him if you want to; he's still up at the bank.''

The big man straightened back off the counter, gazing from one of them to the other. He wagged his head. "I've known you two a long time. I never had any idea you was such a schemin' pair of old coots. An' suppose I hadn't come over tonight?"

"We figured to wait, to give you the chance, an' if you didn't, we was going without you," stated the gunsmith, coming as close to smiling broadly as he ever had. "Now then, you want to go or stay?"

"You'd go without me?" Fogarty exclaimed. "You're crazier than a pair of pet 'coons."

Neither the harness maker nor the gunsmith rebutted that remark. They were relaxed as they watched the lawman and waited for his decision.

A dark man in a baggy coat that looked like he'd slept in it appeared in the doorway. He walked toward the counter, dark eyes restlessly moving. He ignored the lawman and scowled at Hugh Pepperdine. "How long are you two going to stand around here drinking coffee while that six thousand dollars is getting farther away? I said I'd pay for the coach, but they're getting impatient up at the corralyard and so am I."

Hugh chewed, said nothing to the banker, and looked steadily at Marshal Fogarty. Seconds passed before the lawman spoke. "All right. I'll meet you up yonder after I get my gun and my heavy coat." He turned as though the banker were not there and walked out of the shop on his way down to the jailhouse.

McGregor finished his coffee. "Fifteen minutes, Mr. Donner. If you're goin' back up to the yard, you can hand them that sack near the door and ask them to pitch it inside. We're likely to be hungry before morning."

The banker twisted to locate the sack, then turned away with a low growl to leave the shop.

Hugh arose carefully and went back to the lean-to for his shell belt and side arm, his blanket coat and a spare plug of tobacco. When he returned, there was no sign of

McGregor, so Hugh blew down the lamp mantle, limped to the plankwalk, locked the roadway door, and started up in the direction of the corralyard.

There were stars overhead in all directions, close-spaced and emitting unsteady light. There was a scimitar moon whose brilliance reached earth considerably weakened, and there was no sign of clouds although Pepperdine looked for them because it was his feeling that from now on summer heat would fill the days. Clouds might have indicated otherwise.

He stopped just outside the big old palisade gates of the corralyard. They had been open so long they sagged into the earth and probably could be closed only by strenuous effort. Inside, men were idly standing at the heads of an impatient hitch, where a lamp suspended from a pole in the harnessing area shone.

There was a little desultory grumbling among the hostlers. The company's Sheridan representative, a gnome of an individual with little pale eyes and scanty hair that he covered with an oversized hat, was unmistakable in the gloom. So was Pete Donner, with whom the gnome was speaking.

Hugh watched the gunshop. When he saw his friend emerge carrying weapons and having difficulty locking his door without setting them down, he limped over to lend a hand. As they were walking back, Marshal Fogarty came striding up from the direction of the jailhouse, bundled in a leather coat lined with sheep pelt.

The three of them entered the yard together. At once the waiting men came alive. Pete Donner opened a door to the coach and held it until the weapons were inside, then he nodded without speaking and turned toward the roadway. When McGregor and Pepperdine had come to him in the late afternoon with their scheme, he had reacted about as Joe Fogarty had, but being a thoroughly practical man, he had arrived at a conclusion Joe had not thought of: Any action was better than no action, and Donner wanted his money back, even if he had to spend a little to get it.

Also, there were no other suggestions for how to get it back.

About the time Donner had cleared the wide gateway, the whip was on his high seat with the lines in hand, the binders kicked loose, ready to roll. Inside, his passengers said nothing as they arranged their armament and got bundled to the gullet. The old man with the huge hat leaned a wizened face inside, little ferretlike eyes twinkling in poor light as he said, "Hang 'em when you catch 'em. That's how we handled that kind when I rode after 'em. Worthless sons of bitches."

The whip was a seasoned hand. He cleared the far-side log gate without even brushing a hub, then moved smartly out into his southward sashay.

CHAPTER SIX

The Southbound Stage

Steel tires grinding through dust made whispery sounds. The coach was old, so it creaked as well as pitched and yawed. It rode over thoroughbrace springs which, until the advent of steel-leaf springs, had been the cause of most complaints by people who rode stages. Seasickness was not exclusive to ships.

The whip walked his hitch southward out of town and for another long mile and did not boost them over into an easy lope until the horses had been warmed up. After that he settled himself for the rocky ride and let a little slack lie in the lines.

Inside, Pepperdine eased his sore leg around until the seat supported his knee, and watched McGregor shrink down inside his coat until only his nose and eyes showed, turtlelike.

Marshal Fogarty slept.

The road was made tawny-pale by starlight. It went arrow-straight for about two thirds of the distance; farther southward near the terminus of the Sheridan plain it followed a course around upthrusts of scabrous black rock and entered a gently rolling country that presaged high and more uneven country ahead.

The driver made good time without using up his horseflesh. When they reached the sod-roofed way station to change animals, the ones taken off the tongue were fresh enough to go another ten or fifteen miles. But they were taken off anyway, and while the fresh team was being backed into place and hitched, Hugh and McGregor climbed stiffly to the ground to stamp cold feet and gauge the chilly night. There still was not a cloud in sight. "It'll be hot from now on," the harness maker prophesied. His friend gazed at the splatter of stars without commenting.

Marshal Fogarty climbed out, reached inside his coat to scratch vigorously, then walked around where the way-station hostlers and the whip were working.

McGregor and Pepperdine remained near the door on the off side. James dug in a deep coat pocket and held out a handful of shotgun shells that Hugh accepted without a word. McGregor said, "Bird shot," and jerked his head rearward toward the interior of the coach. "The scatter-gun is already loaded. Those two long guns came from England. They're about as well made a set as I've ever run across. I've never shot 'em, but I'd guess they'd hold accurate close to a mile."

Marshal Fogarty returned holding two cups of hot coffee, which he handed to the older men. "There's more in the station," he told them, then said, "One of the men went out to round up loose horses and drive them in this afternoon, and saw a band of distant riders heading southeast from up north. If it's the raiders, then they must have decided not to go back to the road."

Hugh was interested in how close the hostler was to the riders. Fogarty shook his head. "Not close enough to make out much except that there looked to be six or eight of them."

"Any ranches out here?" McGregor asked.

Fogarty was troughing wheatstraw paper to tip in tobacco when he replied. "That's what I asked. They said no ranch headquarters within thirty miles." Fogarty tongued the paper, folded it over, crimped the fire end, and popped the cigarette between his lips. As he was lighting up, the driver sang out, jumping from the ground to the wheel hub on his way to the high seat.

They left the way station at a walk and did not increase their speed for another mile. When the whip whistled up his horses, he held the binders down just enough to avoid jerking his passengers, let them off gradually, and as the horses made steady headway in the direction of Bordenton, the whip mitigated his boredom by playing a harmonica with one hand.

Hugh watched the sky. He owned a pocket watch but had tossed it into a drawer years earlier because he never remembered to wind the thing. He guessed it to be within a couple of hours to dawn or thereabouts. It was getting chillier now, which usually went with nearing dawn light.

McGregor said, "If that was them, the ones the feller back at the way station saw, then they either are ahead of us, maybe in Bordenton already, or they've made a camp down-country a ways and we just might get ahead of them. What do you think, Joe?"

Marshal Fogarty was asleep.

Hugh answered for him. "If they made two night camps, then maybe we could get pretty close to them even though we struck out a day after they robbed the bank. Sort of a trade-off; them restin' overnight and us pushing ahead."

McGregor was thinking of something else. "They got a pile of gall," he said. "Robbin' and ridin' to rob again without changing course or scattering to hide out for a while."

Pepperdine thought it might be something besides gall. "Last time I was up in Bluestem and down at San Luis, neither place had a telegraph. Neither does our town. James, I got an idea we're goin' up against maybe the best there is."

McGregor was not that impressed. "One thing they won't have time to do this trip is have the preacher set up a camp meeting to get everyone out of town before we reach Bordenton."

Pepperdine thought about that. Very likely McGregor had made a true statement, but Hugh was beginning to feel less hostility toward the outlaws and more respect. He'd been hearing about robberies most of his life, and with few exceptions the raiders had ended up propped up dead in front of a store or had been quietly hanged and buried.

There had been several notorious gangs of outlaws— the Youngers, the Jameses, riders who raided with Sam Bass, among others—but even the ones commemorated in songs and poems had ended up shot to death or hanged.

Maybe in time a similar fate would overtake the men he, James McGregor, and Marshal Fogarty were pursuing, but if they got over the line down into Mexico, and had sense enough to stay there for a long time, maybe it wouldn't happen to them.

Fogarty, now awake, cut across the harness maker's reverie. "They got a new town marshal in Bordenton. Someone told me his name is Spencer. If we get there ahead of the outlaws, maybe we can get him to help us set up a trap."

This was not a remark that required comment, so neither of the older men spoke.

The cold was coming inside, and although there were rolled-up leather curtains that could be lowered to cover the open upper halves of both doors, no one made a move to snap them down into place.

McGregor leaned to grope through the flour sack with food in it. He handed out tins of salt beef, and peaches put up in sugary syrup. It required a certain degree of dexterity to open the cans with a knife while trying to anticipate the pitches of the old coach, but hunger was the best of all incentives.

The food had a reviving effect. With false dawn making artificial light along the eastern skyline, the cold reached its peak while the men ate. An hour later, fish-belly gray streaks began to spread along the farthest curve of the uneven distant country eastward. The men settled back to wait.

Hugh thought they were not far from Bordenton. McGregor pushed the flour sack beneath his seat and leaned to examine the guns. The other two watched. Once McGregor glanced up, looking quizzical. "What do you think, Marshal?" he asked.

"About what?"

"The odds."

Fogarty blew out a big breath and looked out a window at the passing cold countryside. "There's nothing very good about them." He faced forward to meet the gunsmith's gaze. "We can likely pick up some help in Bordenton."

McGregor went back to examining the weapons without another word. A half hour later, with the promise of new-day sunlight in the offing, the whip leaned down and yelled, "Rooftops."

They leaned out, but even with increased daylight they saw nothing but horses and countryside. They settled back, quiet and thoughtful. It had been a long night, cold most of the time, and about all that could be said of riding the old coach was that it beat crawling on all fours.

Where the roadway bent around a field of large rocks, some as high as a mounted man and many times thicker, it was finally possible for the passengers to catch sight of town.

They were not as close as they had expected. Bordenton was still a couple of miles ahead. The whip dropped his horses down to a steady, slogging walk so that when they arrived at the corralyard down there they would be cooled out.

The whip called again and gestured with a gauntleted hand. "Riders to the east, out a considerable distance."

McGregor said, "Three. If it's our men, then they've split up."

Pepperdine doubted that it would be the outlaws. "Cowboys," he surmised aloud, and leaned farther out as the road made another twist so that he could see the town better.

There was smoke rising over Bordenton, flattening out at a certain height and hanging there. Without a breath of wind stirring to dissipate it, it probably would not fade out until later in the morning.

The smoke reminded Marshal Fogarty of food. McGregor pushed the flour sack toward him with a shotgun butt.

Hugh wasn't hungry. Neither was the gunsmith. Their full attention was on the town up ahead. One thing appeared clear; the outlaws had not yet raided the place, otherwise there would have been pandemonium in the roadway.

When Hugh mentioned this, McGregor said, "Seems likely, but I'm a lot more interested in knowing where those outlaws are. Sure as hell they're down here."

The whip was letting slack hang in the lines now. He was watching the town come out to him with interest. He lived in Bordenton with his wife and three children. He had a house on a back street east of town. He would not have to take out the next northbound stage for two days. He was looking forward to the rest.

Marshal Fogarty wiped his hands on a large blue bandanna, pushed the sack across toward McGregor with a boot toe, and loosened the two top buttons of his sheep-pelted winter coat. He also freed the bottom three buttons to let the coat hang slack above his holstered Colt.

They entered Bordenton at a dead walk, traces slack, lines loose. Around them the town was coming to life, but some of the stores were still closed, and the ones that were open, such as Bordenton's two cafes and the blacksmith's shop, showed few signs of life.

The passengers gazed out at a quiet town as the whip made a big sashay that temporarily blocked the roadway, which did not matter because there was no traffic anyway, eased up into the corralyard, kicked on the binders, looped the lines, and climbed down as a swarthy, squatty man with a badly pockmarked face came forward calling a greeting to him in Spanish.

The driver answered in the same language and stepped over to free the traces on his side of the hitch while the Mexican did the same on the opposite side.

Hugh got out gingerly and tested his injured leg. It

was not particularly painful unless he moved, walked, or turned with his weight on it. As long as he stood still, there was no pain.

Fogarty climbed out next, followed by McGregor, who brought the weapons with him. The Mexican stared at them, then went back to work without a word.

They carried the guns to the office of the stage company and left them there. The agent was not present. Marshal Fogarty led off across the road in the direction of a sturdy brick building with narrow, barred windows in the front wall that were shaded by a large old poplar tree.

He stopped before entering to turn and look for the bank. It was on the opposite side of the roadway, southward a fair distance. It still had the steel shutters closed across its windows as well as in front of the main doorway. Reassured, beginning for the first time to believe he and his companions had reached Bordenton ahead of the raiders, he opened the jailhouse door, held it for McGregor and Pepperdine, then closed it after him.

The room was empty. No one had lighted the iron stove to take the chill off. There was an untidy desk, and the rack of rifles, shotguns, and carbines was full, with a chain running through trigger guards. Even the wood box had kindling in it. Fogarty said, "Over at one of the cafes having breakfast."

McGregor thought that would be a good idea and went back to the door. "Something hot for a change," he muttered, and swung the door open. "Couple cups of coffee."

In the roadway was a team of jet-black horses hitched to a fine black hearse with glass windows on each side and ornate black curlicues along the top. On each side of the windows black wood carved in the form of heavy draperies shone softly in the early sunlight.

Hugh and Fogarty stopped behind McGregor in the jailhouse doorway as four men in plug hats with black ribbons tied around them emerged from a small store carrying a new pine coffin. Each man was attired in black, and each of them looked properly solemn.

They took the coffin to the rear of the hearse, where it was boosted inside. The doors were closed and a fat man grunted his way up to the driver's seat. He, too, was dressed in black from head to toe. The difference here was that the fat man was properly businesslike but not very solemn. He was the liveryman who owned the hearse; he had been driving it to the cemetery for twenty years and no longer made any effort to maintain the lugubrious expression appropriate to the occasion.

He clucked, the hearse moved northward, and people fell in behind it, mostly in black, forming a large funeral cortege. The roadway was completely quiet.

McGregor said, "Must have been the mayor. Maybe the banker."

Fogarty nodded a little, watching the crowd walking slowly behind the hearse. A freckled youth with a turned-up nose came ambling past, trailed by a black dog of mixed descent. McGregor leaned to tap the boy's shoulder. "Who died?" he asked.

The boy stopped, gazed long at the strangers who looked rumpled, sunken-eyed, and slovenly, turned his head to watch the crowd and the hearse heading northwest beyond town, and said, "Marshal Spencer."

CHAPTER SEVEN

Bordenton

Joe Fogarty's reaction to the boy's information was to look up the road after the funeral procession and shake his head. He hadn't known the defunct lawman but had been counting on his cooperation. Now, watching the slow-moving hearse, he said, "Well, I expect the next thing is to find the mayor."

They went to the nearest cafe, which was about half-full, and had a hot breakfast and coffee. They found out from the cafeman that Bordenton's mayor was also chairman of the town council, and operated the smithy at the lower end of town opposite the public corrals and the livery barn.

They went down there. The blacksmith mayor was a powerfully put-together man of slightly less than average height with testy blue eyes and a bear-trap mouth. He acknowledged Fogarty's introduction, eyed Pepperdine and McGregor, and listened to everything Marshal Fogarty had to say. He turned away once when a tousle-headed, muscular younger man came up drying both hands on a rag to announce that he had finished shrinking tires to a wagon wheel. The blacksmith, whose name was Bert Stiles, said, "Walk up to the corralyard, Sam. There's bound to be someone up there. Tell 'em they can come for them wheels anytime." As the younger man headed for the roadway, still wiping his hands, the blacksmith turned back and said, "You got any proof you're the town marshal at Sheridan?"

Fogarty looked surprised, but he dug out his badge and Bert Stiles looked at it. "All right. If it comes down to it, there'll be folks in town who've been up there; they'll most likely know you." Stiles gazed at the older men, who were more nearly his own age. His gaze was not particularly hostile, but it was certainly reserved as he said, "You gents might go up an' talk to Mr. Sanford at the bank. When he gets back. He went out to the cemetery. Our town marshal got kicked in the head by a mule couple days ago."

Hugh Pepperdine, who had completed his assessment of Bert Stiles, said, "Have you appointed a feller to take his place yet?"

Stiles eyed Hugh steadily as he replied. "No."

"Might be a good idea, don't you expect, Mr. Stiles?"

The blacksmith's eyes hardened on Hugh. "Yep. First we got to bury the dead marshal."

Hugh started to say something else, but closed his mouth and returned the blacksmith's steady gaze without blinking. Hugh was beginning to dislike Bordenton's mayor.

McGregor had a suggestion. "They're out there. I'd bet new money on it. Bordenton is in a direct line from Sheridan. Marshal Fogarty told you how they been raidin' in a beeline due south. There's a town in the hills south of here."

Stiles nodded. "Klingerville."

"Might be a good idea to telegraph them a warning, Mr. Stiles."

The blacksmith turned aside to expectorate, turned back, and said, "If what you gents say is true, you're right, it couldn't hurt. But our telegraph line went dead last night. At the cafe this morning the telegrapher sat next to me. He said every morning he sends out a call signal to other operators in other towns. Routine, he said. This morning he didn't get a single acknowledgment." Bert Stiles was not particularly concerned. "He told me every now an' then a low-flyin' bird'll hit the wires and break 'em, or range animals will rub against the posts until they're pushed so far over the wires break."

Joe Fogarty listened in expressionless silence. When Stiles finished speaking, he turned to exchange looks with Pepperdine and McGregor.

Hugh was carving off his morning chew as he said, "Seems right convenient to me, Mr. Stiles. A gang of outlaws somewhere out yonder an' your telegraph system goin' out of operation at the same time." Hugh got the wad into his cheek, stuck the knife back into the tobacco plug, and offered it to the blacksmith.

Stiles wordlessly accepted, sliced off a chew, handed back the plug and knife, and smiled at Hugh. "Obliged," he said.

It was the first expression Bert Stiles had shown that wasn't unfriendly, and Hugh took advantage of it. "Joe told you how those bastards work. They don't charge in like Comanches shootin' and scarin' everyone out of the roadway. They used a preacher up at our town. They got just about everyone out of town that way."

Bert Stiles and Hugh had established a common ground through the plug of Kentucky twist. Stiles gazed steadily at the harness maker for a moment, then said, "I'll tell you straight out that I been thinkin' about that while we been talking. Your friend here, the lawman, said the same thing. These fellers work their robbery real clever."

Hugh nodded. "They do. Called a camp meetin' up at Sheridan. Down here cut the telegraph line."

Stiles continued to study Pepperdine. "What else I been thinking, friend, is that if they're really that clever . . . I've never seen any of you before, and you boys been on the trail a long time from your looks."

James McGregor bristled. "You think we're part of the outlaw band, for Christ's sake! What would we be tellin' you all this for?"

Stiles switched his attention to the gunsmith. "I got no idea. Unless maybe real clever outlaws would want the mayor to rush out, round up a posse, and go scourin' the countryside while they robbed the bank. Maybe."

James started to snarl a retort, but Joe Fogarty spoke first. "Do you know the whip who drives the southbound stage?"

Stiles nodded. "Sure. Jack Carpenter. He lives over on—"

"Go ask him who he brought down from Sheridan last night, and while you're at it, ask him what happened to the bank up there."

Stiles turned, let fly in the general direction of a box of sand near the forge, missed it, and turned back. He studied big Joe Fogarty for a moment before speaking again. "That'd help," he admitted, eyes narrowing slightly. "Tell you what, gents. I'll go back up to the jailhouse with you first, then send someone to find Jack and fetch him over there. All right?"

Fogarty nodded curtly and turned toward the roadway.

Bordenton's main thoroughfare was empty except for a dusty wagon tied up out front of the general store. A grunting clerk wearing a flour-sack apron was loading the rig with boxes of tinned goods.

The clerk watched four men walking diagonally in the direction of the jailhouse, called "Good morning" to Bert Stiles, and went back to his work.

McGregor entered first, Pepperdine followed him. The last man inside the jailhouse office was Mayor Stiles. He was holding a double-action Colt Lightning gun in his right fist. The men from Sheridan were almost too surprised to wonder where he had had the thing down at his shop. He had not been wearing a holster or a belt— at least they had seen none.

He pointed to a cell-room door with the gun. "First cage down there," he stated. "The door's open. Drop your guns first, gents."

Joe Fogarty was red in the face, but it was McGregor who spoke. "What the hell do you think you're doing? Do you think we'd ride all night in a stagecoach to get down here to warn you if we had in mind robbin' your bank?"

Stiles's reply was curt. "You been tellin' me how clever these outlaws are. Tricked you folks and likely tricked other folks up north. I said, drop the guns!"

Hugh let his old gun fall to the floor first. McGregor's lips were sucked back in anger as he also disarmed himself. Joe Fogarty blew out a noisy breath and lifted out his gun to drop it. "Mister," he said to Stiles, "if they're out there, you're goin' to come up lookin' almighty foolish."

Stiles was adamant. "Drop it," he ordered. "Now then, do like I said; go into the cell with the open door. *Move!*"

They moved.

The cell was one of those prefabricated strap-steel cages made elsewhere and assembled inside the building. They were commonplace in places where jailhouses were old and earlier prisoners had been locked into one big room behind a massive oaken door with a little grilled peephole in the upper half of it.

Mayor Stiles let the six-gun dangle as he locked the steel door and looked in. "Now I'll go see if I can find Jack Carpenter. By the way, any of you gents know other folks down here?"

They didn't. Each of them had visited Bordenton over the years, but none had acquaintances here. Stiles said, "I thought not," and went back up front where they heard him locking the steel-reinforced oaken cell-room door.

Hugh went to the windowless back wall and sank down on a three-legged stool. He looked at his companions, too flabbergasted to say a word. James McGregor was the same way. He perched on the edge of a wooden wall bunk, staring out into the dingy little corridor.

Joe Fogarty paced like a caged lion. He was having real difficulty believing what had happened. When eventually he stopped pacing, he leaned on the front of the cage and spoke without looking around. "That damned idiot. Suppose he don't find the stage driver?"

McGregor made a dour response to that. "Then we set in here an' listen to 'em blow the safe, and the hell with Stiles. I hope he loses his savings."

Hugh finally roused himself. "There's one consolation, gents. After their town gets raided, they can't say we had a hand in it. Locked in here like rats in a trap."

McGregor wagged his head. "Busted telegraph line,

folks all out at the town cemetery. You don't expect they engineered the killin' of the town marshal, do you?''

Fogarty turned. ''Not unless they got an accomplice who is a mule.'' He went to a bunk and sat down. ''They couldn't know about the marshal getting killed.''

McGregor's dourness inclined him to say. ''No. I agree with that. I've always heard the Lord works in mysterious ways. I never heard He particularly favored outlaws. He sure did this time. That was a hell of a procession following the hearse.''

Fogarty rolled a cigarette and lit it. The smoke didn't go anywhere. There was no moving air in the cell room and no windows in the back-wall cells. He softly said, ''Where are they? If they scouted the place, they had to have seen that funeral procession. So what are they waiting for?''

Neither Pepperdine nor McGregor responded. They were both thinking the same thing: how to get out of the Bordenton jailhouse. Right now nothing else mattered.

Fogarty fixed them with a bleak stare. ''You're a sly pair. I'm locked in a jailhouse for the first time in my life because of you two. Now then, let's see you figure a way out of this mess.''

They ignored his indignation. The town was quiet. At least from within the jailhouse, with its lack of windows and massive walls, it seemed that way.

An hour seemed like four. Fogarty paced again, wondering aloud why it was taking the mayor so long to locate the coach driver.

McGregor thought of the arsenal they had brought with them and that was now up in the jailhouse office, where it would be useless if trouble arrived.

Eventually, they heard someone enter the office from the roadway, and waited, almost holding their breath, but whoever it was left and slammed the roadway door after himself.

Hugh said, "It don't take all morning to bury someone."

No one agreed or disagreed.

Once they heard a heavy, large wagon roll north up through town and surmised it was one of the freight outfits that kept towns like Sheridan and Bordenton supplied. The wagon did not stop; its sounds diminished with agonizing slowness for the incarcerated men until they were gone and the almost tangible silence returned.

Fogarty rolled and lit another cigarette, Hugh Pepperdine had a cud in his cheek, and James McGregor arose finally to step to the fretwork of steel in the front of their cell and lean there. A rat half as large as a house cat came up the little narrow corridor from somewhere, stopped to sniff in the direction of Joe Fogarty's smoke, then, instead of fleeing, resumed his jerky trip to the front of the cell, where he reared up on his hind legs and looked at McGregor. The gunsmith looked back and laughed.

That little burst of sound sent the rat scurrying. "Must be a pet," James said absently, looking at where the rodent had disappeared.

Someone entered from the roadway. It sounded like two men. McGregor listened briefly, then turned back to his bunk and sat down, watching the corridor. He had heard a key being turned in a lock.

"He finally found the driver. Now we'll get out of here. I'm of half a notion to hunt up the mayor and bust him in the face."

Pepperdine and Fogarty were not listening to the gunsmith; they were listening as the thick oaken door was opened on grating hinge pins.

Two men came down to the front of the cell, halted, and gazed in with expressionless faces. One was the blacksmith mayor, Bert Stiles. The other man was not the coach driver; he was a heavyset individual wearing a suit coat with a vest. He had a closely trimmed salt-and-pepper beard and a round face with coarse, hooded eyelids above direct dark eyes. The blacksmith spoke. "This here is Amos Sanford, Bordenton's banker."

Fogarty ignored that to ask a question. "Where is the stage driver?"

Bert Stiles replied curtly. "Drunk."

The prisoners stared. Hugh said, "What time is it?"

"Nine o'clock," Stiles replied, and gave thick shoulders a little shrug. "If a man drinks, he's as likely to do it this early in the morning as any time."

The grizzled man with the hawklike eyes said, "I haven't heard of no robbery up at Sheridan."

McGregor looked past the steel straps. "You will, mister. With any damned luck you'll more than hear about it, you'll experience it."

That remark did not sit well with either the blacksmith or the banker. Stiles turned toward his companion. "All right, you've seen 'em."

The banker held up a hand. "I told you, Bert. They do have a lawman up there named Fogarty."

"Is that him?"

The raised hand came down. "I told you I'd seen him when I was up there a few years back. No, he didn't look like this man. He didn't have no beard startin' and he looked . . . I don't think it's him, Bert."

"Then let's go see if they got that telegraph fixed yet."

63

Two men came down to the front of the cell, halted,
and one peered in at the three... behind the bars, the
Sheriff... the three behind the bars, the men was not
...
LALMAR PAGE

CHAPTER EIGHT

The Bordenton Jailhouse

A squatty fat woman, dark and pockmarked, brought
three tin pails of stew and a pan of hot coffee, and bent to
shove them beneath the steel door. She glanced only
once at the prisoners and did not say a word as she stood
upright. Her face was flat with coarse features. After she
departed, Hugh arose to retrieve one of the pails. As he
peered in at the greasy stew, he said, "What was she,
part In'ian or Mex?"

Fogarty and McGregor got their pails, too, without
answering. All three men sat down to eat. Hugh chewed,
looked out where the woman had been, and said, "When
she was a baby someone sure beat her in the face with an
ugly stick."

The stew was hot. It had carrots and potatoes mixed
with pieces of boiled meat. James McGregor announced
out loud that he was afraid to speculate on what kind of
meat it was.

Joe Fogarty said, "Mule meat. I've eaten it before. It's
always stringy like this."

McGregor put his pail on the floor and went after the

coffee. He drank from the pan and passed it around. He was thinking about the banker. "That Sanford feller and Pete Donner up at Sheridan was made from the same mold. I've always had trouble cottoning up to bankers."

Hugh, who had the most philosophical nature of the three, ate all his stew and drank his share of the coffee, then tipped back the three-legged stool until his shoulders touched the wall and discreetly belched behind a raised hand before speaking. "We might as well catch up on the sleep we missed last night."

Joe Fogarty was working up a quirley and scowling as he did so. "What's the matter with the damned blacksmith that he don't pour coffee down that coach driver?"

McGregor's opinion of this was dour. "Why should he? He's already got it fixed in his head that we're outlaws. You can change a lot of things in this world, but once a man gets an idea stuck in his mind, changin' it is just about impossible."

It was midafternoon when the blacksmith returned, glanced quickly, almost furtively, in at the prisoners, produced a brass key, and unlocked the door. Without speaking he jerked his head, signaling for them to precede him up to the office. They watched him close the cell-room door, move around behind the littered table that served as a desk, and fling down the key. He cleared his throat and scowled fiercely at the desktop. Their handguns were on the table. He gestured. "Take 'em," he said.

McGregor glowered. "You got the whip sobered up?"

Stiles nodded curtly, red in the face. "He told me 'n' Mr. Sanford who you fellers are."

"Did he tell you about the bank robbery at Sheridan?"

"Yes. He told us." Finally, the burly man raised his

head. "We got men riding out. If those outlaws are anywhere around, they'll find 'em."

Joe Fogarty holstered his Colt as he dryly said, "Sure they will. A bunch of townsmen raisin' dust in all directions out in plain sight . . . Sure they will."

Stiles did not like the sarcasm. "They've had most of the day to show up. Durin' the funeral out yonder they could have raided us and they didn't. Marshal, we been discussin' it over at the saloon. It's our guess they bypassed Bordenton and kept right on going."

Fogarty was resettling his shell belt and did not reply. Neither did Hugh or James McGregor. Bert Stiles crossed to the roadway door and held it open. He clearly wanted to see the last of his prisoners. As they walked out into late-day sunlight, he pointed toward a cafe across the road. "Supper's on the town council."

Fogarty regarded the shorter, older man, turned, and started across the roadway, knowing that they had just received as near to an apology as they were going to get. He was still smoldering as they sat down at the cafe counter.

When the cafeman appeared, they ordered roast beef with spuds, lemon pie, and black java, and they noticed the black armband on his upper right sleeve. Fogarty asked how the town marshal had died, and the cafeman explained.

"He was a mule man. Now, me, I got respect for 'em. They're supposed to pull things, but Marshal Spencer, he rode mules. Said they was tougher'n horses and a lot smarter. Well, smarter or not, a big *grulla* mare mule he rode. . . . Y'know, he'd shod her fifteen, twenty times. This time when he stepped back to hoist a hind leg she hit him right square between the eyes. You boys ever been kicked by a mule?"

They didn't say whether they had or not. They didn't have the opportunity. Jack Carpenter, the whip who had driven the stage south with them as passengers, walked in, gray as ash, with squinting, watering eyes. He sank down at the counter, called for black coffee, and turned. When he recognized the men from Sheridan, he wagged his head. "I couldn't believe it. Bert's so damned suspicious. Him an' Amos Sheridan. I told him the whole story, about you being town marshal up there, an' about the robbery. They walked out lookin' like kids who got caught with their hands in the cookie jar." The driver reached for the cup that was set in front of him and paused with it in midair. "You fellers goin' to take it up? Sanford was sweatin' blood for fear you would."

McGregor was sitting back as the cafeman leaned over to put a platter in front of him. Joe Fogarty answered the driver, but he, too, was watching the cafeman. "We're not going to do anything until we eat."

The cafeman refilled their cups and lingered in front of the stage driver, looking critically downward. "Got an early start this morning, didn't you, Jack?"

Carpenter looked into his cup as he muttered, "Yeah. Maybe." He did not raise his eyes until the cafeman had disappeared, then he turned a crooked smile toward the men from Sheridan. "He's my wife's brother. Otherwise I'd have hit him."

By the time supper was finished, there were shadows forming along the west side of town. It had not been as hot a day as it could have been for summertime. When McGregor was standing out front of the cafe, he cast a skeptical glance at the sky. There were a few very distant, soiled-looking clouds far to the northeast.

Joe Fogarty said, "Let's go see when the evening coach heads north."

It had already departed, and there would not be another coach out until midmorning the next day. Standing in front of the stage company's office, Hugh eyed a saloon almost directly opposite and nudged McGregor. They struck out through manured roadway dust, and because it was too early for townsmen to appear at the bar, and also because it was not Saturday, when rangemen loped in, the saloon had very few customers.

Four old gaffers were playing toothpick poker near a big iron stove in poor light, and an elegant drummer in a curl-brimmed pearly-gray derby hat, a suit to match, and button shoes that had white uppers, was carrying on a desultory conversation with a bored barman, when McGregor, Fogarty, and Pepperdine walked in.

The barman was also wearing one of those black bands around his upper sleeve. He brought a bottle with three jolt glasses. He smiled and went back up where the traveling salesman was nursing a five-cent beer.

Joe said, "Stuck here for the night."

Hugh did not object. "Better'n sleepin' in another stagecoach."

McGregor was sipping whiskey like it was sarsaparilla and making a study of the somewhat hefty naked lady in a large painting over the back bar. She was trailing a veil over the couch where she was half reclining. McGregor did not hear the discussion about spending the night in Bordenton. When Hugh nudged him, he gave a little start, then scowled at the harness maker. Hugh said, "I asked if you knew where the rooming house was?"

James growled his answer. "At the lower end of town. Used to be down there anyway. Big old shack, looks like maybe it was an army barracks once." He went back to studying the faintly smiling, hefty lady.

They were invited by a rosy-cheeked man with pale, plump hands to sit in on a game of faro and declined. Fogarty eyed the dealer with a hard scowl. It had been his custom for years to run professional gamblers out of Sheridan. Evidently, down here the lawman had taken a more tolerant view.

The Bordenton banker appeared in the doorway, saw who was leaning along the bar, turned abruptly, and departed. Later, with dusk settling, Bert Stiles came in looking different. He was wearing a clean shirt, his face shone from scrubbing, and his hair was painstakingly brushed down both sides with a part down the middle. He offered to stand a round, and Hugh accepted for his friends. Stiles said, "Those fellers who made a sashay beyond town didn't turn up anything. Not even any cold camps." He downed his shot, put silver atop the bar, and said, "We don't want you gents leavin' town with hard feelings. Look at it from where I was. Three strangers lookin' like they been sleepin' in their clothes an' all come in sayin' there was a band of outlaws heading toward Bordenton—"

Fogarty interrupted. "When you was a little kid, did you believe in Santa Claus, Mr. Stiles?"

The blacksmith blinked, then began to redden. "What's that mean, Marshal?"

Joe did not raise his voice nor look up from his shot glass as he answered quietly. "Now an' then I've run into folks who wouldn't believe the Second Coming was at hand even if they heard trumpets and the sky turned all sort of golden."

Stiles, who was not a man of even temperament, turned and stamped out of the saloon.

Hugh stifled laughter. McGregor, who had completed his detailed study of the hefty lady over the back bar, shook his head. "Joe, did you ever hear it said that every man is a fool for at least five minutes of every day?"

Fogarty had indeed heard that. "Yes, for a fact. And that darned old screwt proved it—for six hours."

Two freighters stamped in, large, bearded men wearing heavy shirts of buffalo plaid. They ordered whiskey and settled in sullen silence to drink. No one went near them except the barman, and he was properly deferential. Whatever had annoyed the large, bearded men was still doing so. When the barman lifted the bottle after filling their glasses, one of the freighters caught his arm at the wrist in a grip of steel. The barman grimaced and leaned to put the bottle down. The freighter glared. "You scairt we wouldn't pay, Mister?"

The barman blanched. "No, sir. Never thought about it." He managed a weak smile. "The next one's on the house, gents."

The surly big man showed square white teeth through black whiskers. "The bottle is on the house," he growled.

The old men at the poker table turned to listen and look. The elegant peddler in the gray derby hastily put some coins on the bar and headed for the roadway door.

The barman eyed the bottle. It was nearly full. Drinks sold out of it at two bits a jolt made the bottle's contents valuable. He eyed the pair of cold, closed faces looking directly at him, and raised a hand to brush a sudden showing of sweat beads off his upper lip. "The whole bottle?" he asked feebly.

One of the men in plaid shirts said, "The whole bottle an' maybe one for the road. That'd be right neighborly, wouldn't it?"

Hugh and James were as transfixed as the old men over near the iron stove. Both of them started when a voice from directly behind them said, "Stand away from the bar! I mean it! Both of you!"

The freighters turned in surprise. Joe Fogarty was standing several feet away from the bar, hands loose, face set like stone. This was his element.

The freighters had a moment to consider. One of them straightened up. "Who the hell are you?" he growled.

"A man who don't like bullies." Joe nodded toward the whiskey bottle on the bar. "If you want the bottle, pay for it."

The second freighter moved clear of his friend. He had made his assessment of Joe Fogarty. "We ain't armed," he said.

Fogarty did not acknowledge this statement, he simply reiterated what he said before. "Pay for the bottle!"

The second freighter dug in a trouser pocket for coins, which he put atop the bar. His companion was still eyeing Fogarty coldly. He also eyed Pepperdine and McGregor, both armed, both obviously friends of the big man who had challenged them. He blew out a noisy breath. "Well now, mister, if you'll shed that side arm, we can go out into the roadway and talk this over."

Joe gazed steadily at both men for a long while before speaking. "One at a time," he told the man who had challenged him, then he shrugged mighty shoulders. "You first . . . but you better think it over. I do this for a living, an' I've done a lot of it."

The second freighter, the man who had paid for the bottle, nudged his companion. "Russ, what the hell. Losin' three horses ain't worth all this, too. Let's go."

Fogarty's gazed drifted to the speaker. "What three horses?" he asked.

The second man replied. "We set up camp last night north of here. Hobbled the mules and our three saddle animals. This morning the hobbles of the horses was in the grass an' the horses was gone. We been all day tryin' to track them from muleback.''

"Did you find them?"

"No. What we tracked as far as we could was two riders on shod horses leading three other shod horses. Ours sure as hell.''

"Where did the tracks go?"

The freighter made a wild gesture with one arm. "West of here into a field of rocks a couple hunnert acres wide.''

"Did you find a camp, anything at all?"

"Not a damned thing,'' stated the bearded man, who was eyeing Joe Fogarty with interest instead of his earlier hostility. "Are you the local lawman?''

"No. Not here. Up in Sheridan, north of here.''

That seemed to satisfy the freighters. The belligerent one loosened a little, looked around the room, then back as he said, "Well . . . maybe I was a little hasty.''

Fogarty accepted that as an apology but did not comment about it. The same bearded man asked where the local lawman was, and the barman replied in a strained voice, "We buried him today. We don't have no replacement yet.''

The belligerent freighter looked disgusted. "Fine. No lawman, no posse . . .'' He turned back to the bar and carefully filled his jolt glass. He tipped back his head and dropped the whiskey straight down. He slammed the little glass down and jerked his head at his companion. "Come on. We still got that load for the store up at Sheridan. Let's get away from this damned place.''

CHAPTER NINE

Into the Night

McGregor said, "Joe, it don't have to be connected."

They were strolling toward the lower end of town in the direction of the rooming house. Fogarty was silent for a while. "It don't," he finally agreed. "But those outlaws just darned well might need fresh animals. You can't do what they been doin' forever on the same horses."

Hugh Pepperdine was chewing and let his friends carry the discussion. He was tired. Whether the horse thieves were part of the outlaw band or not did not really interest him a whole lot right now.

But his leg was much better. Evidently, being unable to use it much during their day-long incarceration had helped.

The woman who operated the rooming house squinted at them in poor lamplight, jerked her head, and without a word led them to a room with three wall bunks in it and very little else, except for commode pots and wall pegs for hanging clothing.

She required payment in advance. After she had the

money she left them. They turned up the wick of the small coal-oil lamp she had lighted and looked around. McGregor examined the underside and seams of a mattress. If there was wildlife, he could not see it in the poor light.

As they were kicking off their boots after draping their gun belts and shirts on the wall pegs, Pepperdine tested his bunk, then stretched out atop it. "I've slept worse," he commented, and yawned. "Joe, horse thieves are a nickel a dozen. Seems to me you're ready to attach just about anythin' to those bank robbers."

Fogarty sat on the edge of a bunk having his last smoke of the day. "The blacksmith could be right. They bypassed Bordenton. If I was in their boots, I would. Common sense would tell you not to keep raidin' in a straight line like they did up north." Fogarty ground out his smoke and lay back. "James?"

"What?"

"You ought to get married."

"What!"

"That fat lady in the backbar picture . . ."

McGregor snarled a curse and flung up on his side so that his back was to Joe Fogarty. It was too dark, and his face was hidden anyway, or Fogarty might have seen how red it was.

Sleep arrived shortly after their talking stopped, and it was deep sleep, otherwise Joe and McGregor would have flung boots at Hugh Pepperdine, who snored every time he fell asleep on his back.

Bordenton became very quiet except for a couple of dogs raising Cain at the upper end of town. If the three sleeping men had been awake, they would not have paid any attention. Every night in every town dogs barked, because with the coming of darkness and silence, four-legged foragers crept along back alleys rooting in trash barrels. The more enterprising varmints scouted along the base of faggot-fenced chicken yards. If they could dig inside, they played havoc with roosting chickens.

Ordinarily, town dogs did not continue to bark, or they had quiet periods between barking sessions. The Bordenton dogs did not let up.

It was about midnight, a little past in fact, when something awakened James McGregor. He rose up a little to listen. But it had not been a sound that had awakened him, it had been the bunk he was lying on quivering. In seconds he was wide awake. He called Fogarty, got no response, rolled out groping for his boots, crossed over, and violently shook the lawman.

Joe blinked awake with the gunsmith's face six inches away as McGregor said, "Building shook. You hear me? The building shivered an' woke me up."

Fogarty did not move for seconds, then he came up off the bunk like a man activated by steel springs. He went first to the wall pegs for his gun belt and shirt, dropped the hat on the back of his head, and went back for his boots. "Wake Hugh," he told the gunsmith. "Are you sure, James? I didn't feel anything."

"I'm sure. Like a short earthquake."

Fogarty was out the door rushing toward the front porch by the time McGregor had Hugh Pepperdine awakened. He was still standing out there when the older men emerged from the building. He wrinkled his nose. "You smell anything?" he asked.

Hugh grunted. He had detected the same odor up in Sheridan. "The bank!" he exclaimed, and started toward the middle of town in a limping lope.

McGregor called to Marshal Fogarty. "Fire off a few rounds. Wake the town."

Fogarty kept on running without touching his holstered Colt, but when they were in front of the bank where the burnt-powder scent was strong, he said, "Quick. Around in back."

There was nothing back there. A little dust in the alleyway, a very faint half-heard sound of running horses, nothing else.

Fogarty went over to the rear of the bank, where a door was hanging open, its hasp and big padlock hanging askew. Fogarty drew his handgun and fired off three rounds. The sounds were deafening, and their echoes lingered through the silence. Fogarty led the way inside the bank, where it was too dark to see much until Hugh found a hanging lamp and lighted it. Then there was enough to see. The burnt-powder smell in there was very strong.

A large steel safe bolted into a corner behind the little wooden railing that separated the front of the place from the back part, where several desks and an assortment of chairs were, stood gapingly open. Scattered like confetti were feathers and some kind of wadded-up cloth that had been inside what remained of a number of bed mattresses. The interior part of the bank was a shambles.

There were distant catcalls from the lower and middle part of town. Hugh left the bank and went around to the main thoroughfare, where hastily dressed men were beginning to appear. He hailed them. As they ran up, some carrying shotguns, some with six-guns in their waistbands, all of them puffy-faced and rumpled-looking, Hugh told them what had happened and pointed toward the alley.

One man remained after the others had hurried away. It was the blacksmith mayor, and he was eyeing Hugh with a troubled glare. The harness maker had seen the identical expression on the blacksmith's face before, and said, "Use your head for a change, Mr. Stiles. If we'd raided your bank, would we have fired off rounds or waited around to tell you what happened?"

Bert Stiles went trudging toward the back alley, and as Hugh watched him go, he felt for his plug, gnawed off a cud, and shook his head.

A balding man with an overhanging gut came up with a sawed-off scattergun hooked into the crook of one arm. He stopped at the sight of Hugh. "Who are you?" he asked.

Pepperdine studied the man with the paunch. "One of the fellers who felt the shaking when they blew the safe in there. Who are you?"

"Dennis Morgan. I own the livery barn."

Hugh's eyes narrowed on the fat man. "There is nothing in there but an empty safe, feathers all over hell. You can come back and look around. Right now me 'n' my friends need three good horses."

The fat man stared.

Hugh leaned to tap the liveryman's chest with a rigid finger. "You deaf? Three good saddle animals right now. Fast, friend. Move, damn it! *Move!*"

The liveryman could hear angry voices out in the alley. He hesitated, so Hugh reached out, turned him by the shoulder, and prodded him over the kidneys with his belt gun. The liveryman got the hint and went lumbering back the way he had come. Down in front of the jailhouse he stopped once to look back. Hugh yelled at him, and the fat man continued southward in what was probably for him a run.

More people appeared in the chilly, dark roadway, some aimlessly wandering, calling questions back and forth, some resolutely approaching the bank.

Joe and the gunsmith appeared. Hugh told them about

the horses and led off southward at a stiff trot. In front of the jailhouse McGregor stopped, went inside, and returned with a shotgun, two long-barreled rifles, and a sagging pocket of shells. He had to run to reach the livery barn, where Fogarty and Pepperdine were already leading saddled animals out toward the roadway. McGregor passed out weapons, kept the shotgun for himself, ignored the owl-eyed look he got from the fat liveryman, grabbed the reins from the man's hand, and hastened after his friends.

As they were mounting, Burt Stiles yelled at them from up near the center of town. They ignored him, but the liveryman didn't; he ran to the middle of the roadway and yelled back.

Joe Fogarty led off at a fast walk. It was difficult to be restrained with the scent of freshly roiled dust in the face, but he favored the livery horse until it was safe to boost it over into a lope.

The night was moonless, chilly, and totally empty. Twice they halted to detect sound and failed both times. Hugh cursed under his breath because it was too dark to read signs. He thought the outlaws would use the stage road. They could make much better time that way than running across country in the dark, risking a broken neck or worse. His leg began to ache after a half hour of horsebacking. He ignored it.

Joe Fogarty was on a good trail and did not look back to see where his companions were. Like Hugh, he had to ride balancing a long-barreled rifle across his lap. Even if there had been saddle boots, they would not have been deep enough to accommodate rifles, only carbines.

The chill increased. As long as the pursuers had the scent of dust in their faces they were aware of little else, cold included.

There would be other riders somewhere behind them.

There would also be an anguished banker and a chagrined blacksmith mayor. Bordenton would be in an uproar.

Fogarty finally hauled down to a walk. Hugh and James came up on either side of him. The big lawman squinted dead ahead as he said, "This time, by gawd, if they get clear they're goin' to earn it."

Hugh Pepperdine, the old rangeman, said, "Yeah. So may we if they hear us coming an' set up a bushwhack. In this kind of rocky country that's easy to do."

The warning had little effect on Marshal Fogarty, a man of unalterable resolve once he was on a good trail.

They were still resting the animals at a walk when they heard wolves calling back and forth across a considerable distance out to the west somewhere. Hugh sprayed amber before saying, "We know they didn't go over there anyway."

Fogarty's reply was terse. "They used the stage road sure as hell. If they leave it, won't be until they see us comin' after dawn or unless they find a better route through the hills up ahead."

McGregor, who had been riding grimly silent, rolled up the collar of his shirt and buttoned it. "How far before we get off this blasted country?"

"Five miles," stated Fogarty. "More or less. Don't worry, we'll reach the hills before daylight."

Pepperdine rode, watched ahead, gauged the night, estimated the time, studied the flawless sky with its rash of flickering white stars, and wagged his head over the Bordenton raid. "No imagination," he eventually said, as much to himself as to his companions. "Men got no imagination who use the same system to raid banks and stay to the same course afterward."

Joe Fogarty cast a jaundiced look at the harness

maker. "It's worked. Every blessed time it's worked; you can't fault them for that."

The roadbed became pebbly with fewer washboard ruts and more pale rock beneath a sheet of dust. McGregor worried about the sounds they made as their shod animals rattled stones and came down hard over rock. Noise carried a considerable distance at night.

Fogarty did not relent in his total resolve until the land began to tilt. Then he rode more often at a walk while straining to pick up sounds or to sight movement.

From this point on they were in rough, crumpled low hills, mostly of bare rock as pale as exposed bones. There were few trees but a fair amount of underbrush. It was ideal ambush country.

The open land had been perilous enough, but they'd had the advantage of darkness back there. Now, penetrating deeper through the scrub hills, a scarcely noticeable but very real lifting of the gloom increased visibility somewhat, which meant that it would do the same for anyone watching a back trail.

Pepperdine studied the country—as much of it as he could discern. He had been this far south a time or two, but it had been as a stagecoach passenger many years earlier. He remembered almost nothing about it. But he had not always been a harness maker either. He raised his right hand to point with. "There's a trail, Marshal. Looks like it might lead to that highest knoll to the southeast." He did not say any more. He did not have to. Marshal Fogarty left the road, picked up the trail, and rode ahead. It was a good trail and very old, but it was also narrow. They rode in single file.

McGregor thought out loud that they were taking a long gamble on being able to see for many miles atop that knoll, and sacrificing the haste they could be making on the stage road to do it. He was correct, but as Hugh reminded the gunsmith, even if they saw nothing more than dust up ahead, it would have been worth it because they would then know there would be no ambush.

Dawn was approaching with a steadily widening band of daylight in the east. By the time Joe reached the top of the knoll and swung off to squat and study the surrounding country, it was possible to see movement if it was no more than a mile or so distant.

Hugh leaned across a saddle seat, his jaws motionless as he very methodically studied blocks of southward country for movement. When he finally saw it, he grunted, spat, and resumed masticating. "They ain't on the road. Watch to the southeast maybe a mile or such a matter on our left." He spat. "They sure make good time."

CHAPTER TEN

A Long Day

It did not occur to any of them that the dust they watched might not belong to the outlaws. If it had occurred to them, they would have been skeptical that it could have been anyone else; no one in his right mind except renegades and their pursuers would be out in such godforsaken country at this time of the early morning. Moreover, that dust was moving right along.

Hugh watched and chewed, and said, "I'll tell you one thing for a damn fact, gents. There was never a horse foaled who could keep that up."

From this point on the pursuit was slow. It had to be; even in the irregular flat places down through the rocky hills, footing was treacherous.

They were still riding when the sun popped out of the east like the seed popped out of a grape. Sunlight drenched everything except the deepest passes through the crooked, rugged hill country.

Their livery animals were holding up well, which was a source of gratification. Evidently, the fat man back yonder had taken Hugh very seriously about providing good stock.

They split up. Joe Fogarty and James McGregor rode on each side of the heights, and Hugh rode down in the canyons. He could only guess where he was going by watching the other two. If they veered west he knew the canyon he was in was going to bend around in that direction shortly.

They did not call to one another. The only sound for a solid two and a half hours was made by horses. McGregor's scattergun was easy to manage, but those long-barreled rifles were a pure affliction for Pepperdine and Marshal Fogarty. There was no way to pack them except across the lap, and it became distinctly uncomfortable after so many hours.

Hugh's chewing plug got very small. On top of that, he was both thirsty and hungry. When he had to ride through direct sunlight it was downright hot. Not a breath of air stirred down where he was. Up above, only an occasional vagrant little breeze dried sweat on Fogarty and McGregor.

The pair on the heights squinted to keep the dust in sight. When it suddenly ended, Joe Fogarty scratched his head. They were closer now, which meant that, since they had been unable to make very good time, the outlaws must have been slackening off.

When Hugh came across a little trickling spring that emptied in a shallow place among the rocks, his friends came down to tank up their animals. McGregor told Pepperdine the dust had disappeared. Hugh gazed up from rubbing his knee. "Maybe they're crossin' a field of rocks. In this country it wouldn't surprise me none."

Fogarty impatiently and grudgingly let the horses rest. When he thought they'd been relaxed long enough, Joe led off again, but this time they all three remained down in the crooked little canyons.

Afternoon arrived. They were still plodding, mostly in hot shade, occasionally in hotter sunlight. McGregor squinted at the harness maker. "I remember my grandfather saying it never got really hot in Scotland."

Hugh accepted that. "Why did he leave?"

McGregor faced ahead again. "I'm not sure. I think it had to do with something he did the English didn't like."

Joe Fogarty made a curt, revealing statement about his own forefathers. "There was lots of things the English didn't like. In Ireland, where my father came from, they didn't like just about everything."

A scrubby dog-coyote came out of a shallow place in the rocks, saw the riders, and didn't even look back. He ran so fast he barely touched the ground every ten or twelve feet.

Fogarty was disengaging a dog tick from the back of his neck as he watched the coyote flee. When he finally loosened the tick, he looped both reins, positioned the tick between thumbnails, and exerted pressure.

When the execution had been completed, Joe said, "Now we know what lives in this kind of country."

The sun was beginning to slant away. Up above it may also have been losing some of its heat, but down in the rocky canyons it was not possible to tell.

"Eight to three," Pepperdine suddenly drawled.

Joe picked that up immediately. "With us having the drop."

"Yeah, so far, but that'll change. If there's a posse from Bordenton back yonder, unless they got a sign reader along, they're goin' to go chargin' right down that damned road without any idea where we turned off," Pepperdine said.

The canyons began to tip upward and the topouts began to look less ragged and rough. Some air came up from the south. It smelled cool.

Hugh took the lead and found another piddling spring, where they watered the horses and pushed on again. The day was waning by the time they could tell the low hills were about to give way to a different kind of country.

Hugh gigged his horse into a fast walk. About a half mile ahead he drew rein in a stand of white oaks, swung to the ground, and sat down to await the arrival of his companions.

Dead ahead was range country. There were no buildings as far as he could see, but there could have been because the land rose slightly into long, thick landswells that seemed occasionally to reach a height of ten feet. It was the custom in open country like this to put the backs of buildings against one of those lifts of land so that howling winter winds could be at least partially blocked.

Fogarty came up and dismounted. McGregor did the same but leaned in horse shade after loosening the cinch while he studied the southward flow of brushy grassland. "No wonder they quit making dust," he mused aloud. "I'll tell you what I think: They're out there somewhere. They got to rest those horses and maybe they figure they're far enough ahead of any pursuit to slack off for a while."

Joe Fogarty rolled and lit a thin quirley. "But where?" he asked softly. "Sure as hell, as we ride down out of here they're going to see us coming." He waved a thick arm. "Anything moving down there would stand out like a sore thumb."

Hugh's eyes were half closed. "I'm gettin' too old for this," he complained, was briefly quiet, then raised a long arm. "Cattle. Watch down there due south. Wait, you'll see it."

Eventually they did, and as McGregor was peering from eyes that were pinched nearly closed, he said, "An old man like you isn't supposed to have that kind of eyesight. I've noticed it before."

Pepperdine straightened up a little. "An old man like me, you screwt? I'm younger'n you."

McGregor batted at deer flies. "How old are you?"

Hugh's eyes jumped away and back. "Younger'n you. That's all you got to know."

McGregor turned his head slowly. "Hugh, by golly, you don't know how old you are, do you?"

Pepperdine struggled up to his feet without answering, without even looking at the gunsmith. He gauged the position of the sun, looked southward, watched those distant cattle moving placidly along as they cropped grass, then made a second study of the reddening sun where it was descending in the west. "Marshal," he said, "we're in a tough spot. If we ride out there in daylight, they're goin' to see us. If we ride out there after dark, they're not goin' to see us, and we're not going to see them."

Fogarty replied almost absentmindedly. "No. But if they're out there, if they haven't struck out again, we just damned well might smell their cooking fire."

Pepperdine considered the younger and larger man for a while in stoic silence, then he grunted and sat back down. Few things in this world were harder for a man Hugh's age to tolerate than for a much younger man to so casually mention how a difficult problem could be resolved. Hugh groped around for the tattered remnant of his plug and bit off a portion of it.

"Maybe they'll make a cold camp," he said.

Fogarty acknowledged this possibility. "Maybe. I think I would even if I thought I was so far ahead of pursuit I was safe. But they got horses, and horses nicker when they pick up the scent of other horses."

Hugh gave it up with a sigh. The next time he spoke was after the gunsmith mentioned that it had been a long time since he'd had anything to eat. "Care to try some chawin' to take the edge off your appetite?"

McGregor gave his friend a vinegary look, said nothing, and settled into a cross-legged posture on the ground, mostly in tree shade, with the shotgun leaning against a nearby boulder.

Joe Fogarty smoked, thought, and waited. He was satisfied the outlaws were out there. It had been imperative that they rest their horses after their long, flinging rush away from Bordenton. What bothered Joe most was sitting like this after all that hard riding to get close. For all he knew, his guess could be wrong; the outlaws could still be riding south. If they were, then they were going to escape, because unless Joe and his companions could find a place to get fresh mounts, they would be unable to keep up the horse race.

However, Joe was convinced the renegades were out there, hiding somewhere, resting, maybe divvying up the bank loot from Bordenton. What the flight and pursuit had boiled down to was a horse race, and somewhere along the way both the pursued and the pursuers had to rest their animals.

But he had a nagging doubt, which made him roll and smoke one quirley after another.

Those cattle they had watched earlier had been grazing along northward, so that even with dimming daylight it was still possible to see them. Nothing else held the attention of the three men. Nothing else was moving as far as they could see, until a horseman appeared as though he'd come up out of the ground.

He had ridden up over the topout of one of those rolling landswells and was heading in an easy lope in the direction of the cattle.

The three watchers became immediately alert. A horseman meant a ranchyard somewhere in the distance. Hugh jettisoned a cud and leaned for support on the long-barreled rifle as he watched the horseman make a big sashay far out and around the cattle so he could come up in front of them, cut off their northward drift, and head them in a different direction.

McGregor, ever pragmatic, said, "Now then, we can tail him or, better yet, watch to see which way he goes, and go the same way after dark. There'll be fresh animals."

They did not wait until dark. They rationalized that when early dusk arrived, shortening visibility, and they could not see the rider, he would be unable to see them.

The horses were a little tucked up, which was inevitable, but they'd had a long rest, had the pleats taken out of their guts from picking grass, and went down out of the rugged low-hill country with surefooted ease.

Joe was in the lead until they reached grassland. Down there they could ride abreast. McGregor, thinking of those cattle that they could no longer see, said, "Now's when a man needs a good dog," meaning a dog would pick up the cattle scent.

No one disagreed with him.

The older men had grumbling innards, but Joe Fogarty, who was larger and heavier than either Pepperdine or McGregor, and therefore should have felt hunger more acutely, seemed impervious to it. Hugh watched the big man's back and softly shook his head. In the length of time he'd known the lawman, he thought he'd figured out just about everything there was to figure out. Evidently not; Fogarty rarely spoke now and never once looked back. His mind was locked on to what he wanted fiercely to believe was up ahead, and not even hunger was going to interfere with that. Joe had become a very stubborn individual.

They loped for almost a mile and were going up the north slope of one of those rolling swells of land, when a lowing cow sounded so close all three riders yanked back to a halt, reaching for weapons.

McGregor jutted out his jaw. "Down the other side of this ridge."

He was correct, but until they swung off, set their hobbles, and crept ahead, rifles in hand, they were not sure. Other cows bawled, their sound signifying to men who had been around livestock most of their lives that the cattle were uneasy, the way driven cattle are.

Fogarty got down in the grass near the rim with Hugh and James on either side. He glanced briefly at them, nodded, and began crawling. It proved to be an excessive precaution, but they did not know that until they were able to lift their heads, lizardlike, and look down into the broad swale below.

The cattle were down there, and so were two men, one dumping his saddlery in the grass, the other one making a stingy little cooking fire out of dry twigs that had been gathered elsewhere, because there were no trees in sight. He was feeding sticks into the little fire as if they were gold.

His companion called something, and the kneeling man at the fire laughed. When he called back, the watchers could hear each word. "He's entitled to be right once in a while, the cranky old cuss."

McGregor eased his weapon ahead in the grass. On Fogarty's opposite side Hugh did the same. He also leaned to whisper to the marshal, "When you hallo to them, make it good. One gunshot out here will carry to hell and back."

Fogarty nodded without taking his eyes off the cowboys. He waited until they were both hunkering near the little fire, saddlebags at hand, then he raised up slightly and sang out.

"Evening, gents. Now, just set still. No . . . don't touch your weapons. We're hid from you but we can see you clear as can be." The watchers waited until the initial astonishment passed and the rangemen relaxed slightly, looking along the rim, seeking the body connected to the voice that had hailed them.

Fogarty called again. "Toss the handguns away. Never mind whispering, just do like I said. We're not here to make you any trouble. Shed the guns!"

The cowboys obeyed. One of them had a droopy handlebar mustache. The other one looked much younger. He was the one Fogarty watched closest. The older man was already beginning to relax. Fogarty addressed the older man. "You with the mustache, get your friend settled. We don't want to shoot him."

The older man said something, and his companion finally loosened a little. They both watched as big Joe Fogarty arose slowly, rifle pointing at them. Neither cowboy moved. Joe smiled in the dusk. "Now, just set easy."

Hugh and James waited until Fogarty was starting down toward the little supper fire, then followed him. It was McGregor's shotgun that impressed the cowboys most.

When the trio was within range, the older man said,

"Whatever it is you fellers want, we don't have it. Not five dollars between us."

Fogarty halted opposite them. They had to tip their heads to look at him. Joe was an impressive, large man. He grounded his rifle and sank to one knee. "Something to eat, for openers." Then he told them who he was and who his companions were.

CHAPTER ELEVEN

Signs of Trouble

The saddlebags contained food for two men for two days and they had been hunting those lost cattle for one day, so what remained, while it was better than nothing, did not fully satisfy anyone's hunger.

The man with the droopy mustache said his name was Roger Ames. His companion was Billy Howe, the son of the man who owned most of this grass country, and whose ranch was about seven miles southeast, and west of the coach road leading from up north down to a place called Klingerville.

Joe showed them his badge, tucked it away, and rolled a smoke as silence settled. After lighting up, he addressed the older rider. "Six or eight men riding together. They came down here this afternoon."

Roger Ames glanced at his companion and solemnly inclined his head. "I told you, Billy." Then he looked back at Marshal Fogarty. "Who are they; what did they do?"

"Robbed three banks beginning in Colorado and

ending up back in Bordenton. They killed a man in Sheridan. You saw them?''

Ames was trying to light a stubby little pipe with a glowing twig from the fire and did not reply, but the youth did. "Yeah. This afternoon. About midafternoon. They was a fair distance off, but they were making good time and there was about that number of them.''

"They didn't stop?" McGregor asked.

The youth shook his head. "Roger said they'd be renegades of some kind, an' I guess he was right.''

Hugh asked which direction the outlaws had taken, and both the cowboys stared at him as the identical thought struck them both. Ames finally said, "Southeast. Gawddammit, our yard is right in their path.''

Hugh spat amber before making a dry comment. "And they need fresh horses real bad, Mr. Ames. Who is at the ranch?"

"The old man, Billy's grandpaw, his paw, and an old Messican that does chores and hauls in wood an' water.''

Hugh watched the pair of cowboys. Ames was biting hard on the stem of his little pipe. Billy looked about half sick. He said, "Jesus," and rose to his feet with the suppleness of the very young.

Hugh stopped him from turning toward the hobbled horses. "Hold it. We'll all go an' you won't go ahead. We'll go together. You can show us the way. Billy, runnin' your horse to death won't help anybody.'' Hugh nudged Joe Fogarty and got stiffly to his feet. "James an' I'll fetch the horses.'' Fogarty nodded, watching the distraught youth. He and Roger Ames were like statues. Whatever the older rider was thinking was his business. Joe was thinking that no amount of haste covering the seven miles to the ranchyard was going to change anything. If the outlaws had burst into the yard down there seeking fresh animals, and if the men down there had put up any resistance, the consequences would have happened at least an hour earlier, and at the most three hours earlier.

He pointed to the ground and said, "Sit back down. Pick up your guns, both of you. Billy, you listen to me. Our animals will just about get us to your yard. Unless those bastards turned loose whatever riding stock they didn't take, we'll get 'em. . . . We got enough to worry about, we don't need you chargin' down there like a drunk In'ian."

The youth holstered his six-gun and stared into the fire. If dusk had not been deepening the last half hour, Joe would have seen how white his face was and how twisted was his expression.

Roger Ames emptied his little pipe, arose to scuff dirt over the dying supper fire, and walked out to bring in their horses. He was rigging them out when Hugh and James returned.

Not a word was said when they struck out with Billy in front. The cattle watched their departure; then, bovine-like, grunted down to chew their cuds and eventually to sleep.

They made good time without abusing the horses. Roger Ames watched the youth go ahead and quietly told Hugh that Billy was his nephew, that Billy's mother had been his sister, and that she had died four years back. Since then Roger, his paw, and grandpaw and the old Mexican named Carlos had mothered Billy.

Hugh was chewing his last shred of plug tobacco. He listened, nodded, and after a decent interval asked about the ranch. It was very large, Ames said, and ran about three thousand cows. They'd been looking to hire cowboys since early springtime without much luck. He and Billy had been riding for a solid six weeks hunting strays. That little bunch back yonder was their most recent find, but Roger thought there had to be at the very least another couple hundred head out there somewhere.

"Unless we can hire another five, six men before the fall gather, we're goin' to be in trouble. Grandpaw tried, but he's real old. Billy's paw ain't a spring chicken, so it's been the two of us." Roger glanced at Hugh. "Usually there's riders passin' through over at Klingerville, but so far we haven't been able to hire any. Billy's paw just got back yestiddy. The best he could do was three Mexicans. They said they'd come out in the next few days." Ames shrugged. "Maybe they'll show up an' maybe they won't."

Billy was sitting erect in his saddle looking into the descending night. McGregor rode up beside him to ask how much farther.

Billy answered without turning his head. "About a mile an' a half . . . You hear anything?"

McGregor hadn't heard anything and he'd been listening for the past hour. But he did not want to add to the boy's agony, so he said, "You got dogs at the yard?"

"A couple of old ones," Billy answered. "One's deaf and the other one can't see real good. My paw's had them since they was pups." The lad suddenly faced McGregor. "You been on their trail since they raided Bordenton?"

McGregor nodded.

"Without food?"

"Nor sleep."

"Then if they're not at the yard, if they're already gone on fresh horses, how in hell do you expect to keep after them?"

McGregor gave one of his wintry little smiles. It was

hidden from the staring youth by night gloom. "I don't know. We'll just do it, is all."

Roger Ames came up on Billy Howe's off side. "Stay here with these gents," he told the boy, and gigged his mount over into a lope. Billy raised his left hand with the reins in it and McGregor leaned, caught his wrist, and forced the hand down.

Billy met the gunsmith's gaze with a fiery look. McGregor released the wrist and was straightening in the saddle when he said, "If you rush ahead now, you'll likely get your partner killed. If they're still at the yard."

There was not a sound for almost fifteen minutes as the men from Sheridan and the agonized youth plodded along. They were close enough now not to need haste. In fact, haste could be the death of them if those outlaws were up ahead.

Hugh was thinking of an ambush again. But McGregor grunted disagreement when the harness maker mentioned it. "If they're still at the ranch, I'll buy you a new hat," he said, and Pepperdine answered dryly:

"I don't need a new hat, I need a new knee."

"It's botherin' you again?"

"It's never stopped bothering me, James. Mostly though, except when we lope, it's not too bad. But I'll tell you one thing, the next time someone raids Pete Donner's damned bank, I'm goin' to lock up the shop and stay out of sight."

McGregor was not listening. An eerie shadow was approaching from the east at a dead walk. When they met it, the ghost turned out to be Roger Ames.

They stopped when Ames held up a gloved hand, settled himself in the saddle, and said, "They're at the yard."

No one had really expected that. Fogarty frowned. "Are you certain? Did you see them?"

"I saw seven rigged-out fresh horses tied to the rack in front of the barn an' a light at the main house. And someone's been cookin' because you can smell it when you get to the edge of the yard."

Hugh jettisoned the last of his chewing tobacco. He was relieved, in a way, and in another way he was not relieved. The pursuit had been long, hard, and seemingly endless. He had become accustomed to it. Now it was going to end. He leaned on his saddle horn looking at the cowboy with the droopy mustache. "What does it look like to you?"

Ames pulled absently at his mustache before answering. "You fellers know more about these men than I do, but if they been running as long as you say, why then I'd guess they got the fresh animals all right, and they ate a fill, and what with the house being hot an' all from the cooking, and maybe with them believing nobody is close behind them, they could be catching up on some of the sleep they've missed." Ames looked from man to man. "That's a pure an' simple guess."

Hugh nodded as he said, "It'd help if you're right, but these aren't greenhorns, Mr. Ames. I wonder if they'd all bed down at the same time. Supposin' they got a man or two skulking around somewhere keeping watch?"

Joe Fogarty, who had been silent up to now, eased to the ground and stepped to his horse's head. The other men followed his example. Joe said, "Lead off, Mr. Ames. Keep close to your horse's head. Whether they're sleeping or not, if one of our horses whinnies, horses down in the yard will likely whinny back. That's all it will take."

Billy would have led his horse up beside his uncle's if

Joe hadn't stopped him with a growl. He told the youth to stay back with McGregor. He did not want someone who didn't shave yet up front as they approached the yard. Nor did he much want him behind him if there was shooting.

Hugh Pepperdine limped and occasionally used the long-barreled rifle as a walking staff. James McGregor strode beside him, silent and grim. The only thing he said was spoken when rooftops and tall trees became visible through the moonless night. "You're right. You're too old for this, and so am I."

Pepperdine neither looked to his right nor commented. The scent of cooked food lingered in the air. Hugh was not quite as hungry as he had been before midnight, but he was damned close to it.

Ames and Fogarty halted. When the others came up, Ames pointed toward the orange square of light directly southward. Fogarty nodded without speaking. Either someone was still awake at the main house or the lamp had been deliberately left glowing even though the outlaws were sleeping. Fogarty grounded his rifle and leaned on it.

"Hugh, can you and James sneak around and come up through the barn, get those saddled horses led down inside, an' pull the outfits off them?" he said.

Pepperdine's reply was cautious. "We can sure try." He and McGregor handed the reins of their livery animals to the others. Hugh left the long-barreled rifle with Marshal Fogarty and limped in the wake of the gunsmith.

They were cautious. Just once did they put their heads together. That was when Hugh said, "Why unsaddle 'em? Why not just turn them loose out back?"

McGregor did not respond.

The Howe ranch's barn had been painstakingly built of logs hauled from only God knew where. It was old, weathered to a uniform corpse-gray, and cast a massive dark shadow against the less-dark night.

McGregor got to the rough rear wall and stopped there to listen. Hugh put all his weight on his sound leg. They were straightening up to move again when McGregor flung out an arm to stop Pepperdine, who was behind him.

Hugh leaned forward. "What did you hear?"

McGregor's whisper was barely audible even at close range. "Didn't hear anything. Sniff the air."

Hugh sniffed. "Tobacco smoke!"

James jerked his head. "Inside the barn."

Hugh looked over several sheds and outbuildings. One was a large three-sided woodshed chock-full of pine rounds stacked one atop the other. He tapped the gunsmith's shoulder, jutted his jaw in the direction of the wood shed, and went limping over there. McGregor watched with a little scowl.

When the topmost round of pine toppled and rolled. Hugh hid quickly behind another pile, and James McGregor faced the barn's doorless rear opening, shotgun held belly-high in both hands. He did not cock it, not even after a gaunt, rumpled, tall man appeared in the opening looking out where the pine round had rolled.

The man was smoking a brown-paper cigarette as he studied the round and the shed from which it had fallen. McGregor scarcely breathed as the tall man walked out of the barn toward the woodshed. If he had looked to his right, he would have seen the gunsmith. He was looking at the woodshed when McGregor deliberately hauled back one shotgun hammer, then the other one.

The tall man froze.

Hugh limped out of the shed, six-gun in hand. The outlaw dropped his smoke, looked at Pepperdine, then very slowly turned his head until he could see the other old man against the barn with a shotgun aimed directly at him.

Hugh barely raised his voice when he said, "Lift out the gun an' drop it. . . . Good. Now get belly-down on the ground, hands shoved out above your head."

The gaunt man obeyed without even a grunt, but as Hugh limped close enough to kick the gun away, the gaunt man moved like a cat, caught Hugh's boot, and wrenched so hard Hugh went over backward with a startled squawk.

The outlaw hurled himself atop the harness maker, trying desperately to get Hugh's handgun. McGregor ran at him at the same time Hugh swung a roundhouse blow that missed by a foot, and the outlaw hauled back to swing his own fist. He hit Hugh high in the chest, hauled back, and struck him again, this time a grazing blow up alongside the head.

Hugh tried to bring his uninjured leg up hard and fast, but the tall man avoided injury by twisting to one side as he aimed another blow. Hugh tried to twist his head. The blow plowed across his cheek, temporarily dazing him.

McGregor swung the shotgun barrels, hit the outlaw near the temple, and the gaunt man collapsed without a sound across Pepperdine.

McGregor angrily kicked the outlaw off his friend and helped Hugh sit up. He said, "You all right?"

Hugh scowled while gingerly feeling his injured cheek. "Good thing you pulled that son of a bitch off me, or I'd have killed him."

CHAPTER TWELVE

Luck Never Lasts

They took the time to lash their captive at the ankles with his shell belt and secured both arms behind his back with his britches belt. They stuffed the man's soiled handkerchief into his mouth and tied it there with his neckerchief, then left him, entered the barn, went up through until they saw the dozing horses, and halted briefly. Hugh's cheek was hot and swelling. McGregor's heart was still pounding. He looked over his shoulder. "Wait here. I'll bring the horses in one at a time. If anything goes wrong, use your handgun." McGregor leaned the shotgun aside and walked toward the tethered horses.

They eyed him with candid interest, but did not offer to pull back nor shy as he untied them one at a time and led them inside for Hugh to work on.

The distant watchers saw this happening. Fogarty made a bleak smile and spoke to Roger Ames. "They'll be afoot. But having the drop on them isn't goin' to last forever. Is there a way to get inside the house without raising the dead?"

Ames pulled on his mustache. "There's seven of 'em

in there, Marshal. There's me 'n' you, Billy, and those two old gents."

Joe sighed. "And darkness, Mr. Ames. Otherwise we can sit down and wait, and that'll cost us what advantage we got."

"Yes. Billy and I can lead you around behind the sheds and get to the rear of the house." Roger Ames did not sound hopeful. "Y'know, Marshal, all of us shootin' inside that house is going to put an awful lot of lead in a fairly small place."

Fogarty watched McGregor lead inside the last of the saddled horses before turning to go around behind the barn as he and Hugh had done. Billy saw the unconscious outlaw first. He picked up the man's six-gun, rammed it into his waistband, and waited until Hugh and James came out to them. Then Billy said, "Follow me."

They had no difficulty passing down the west side of the big yard. Billy led them out of sight of the house, using darkness as well as outbuildings to conceal their passage.

They were hesitating behind the spring house before making the final crossing toward the west side of the main house, when a dog barked up on the long porch that had been built across the full length of the house.

Hugh swore. Barking dogs in town at night were to be expected and usually did not arouse people, but on an isolated ranch a barking dog was a clear alarm.

Billy looked at his uncle as he said, "Old Jed."

Ames nodded, watching the front of the house. From the beginning he had not liked this idea of stalking the house. Now he liked it a lot less, especially when that steadily glowing parlor lamp began to cast shifting shadows. Someone was not only not asleep, but was now using the lamp to grope through the rooms along the front of the house.

Ames turned toward Marshal Fogarty. Joe was motionless. Behind him Hugh Pepperdine was gently probing the swelling on his face. McGregor started to say something when a door creaked in the darkness up ahead.

Whoever he was, he had left the lamp behind. They knew he was warily moving from the parlor to the long porch, but beneath its solid roof he was invisible to them.

Ames eased back soundlessly to the shelter of the spring house with the others following. Billy remained at the corner of the outbuilding, peering in the direction of the porch.

A match flared over there and swiftly died. Moments later the aroma of tobacco smoke reached to the spring house. Fogarty stepped back to look in the direction of the barn. He could barely make out the tierack. From the porch it would be even harder to see.

If the smoker could see that those saddled horses were no longer out there, he would need nothing more to rush inside and rouse his friends. Outlaws became like Indians; their lives depended upon being extremely alert and constantly suspicious.

Hugh sat down with his sore leg pushed out front. McGregor alternately looked down at him and over to where that scarlet-tipped quirley would flare, then fade, as the smoker inhaled and exhaled.

It was a tense moment. If the outlaw had emerged from the house in his stocking feet, he probably would not leave the porch. If he had his boots on, he just might decide to go down and look at the horses that had been left rigged and ready for immediate flight at the first suspicion of trouble.

Ames's sudden sharp intake of breath carried no farther than where his companions stood, but it was sharp enough to bring their attention back from the porch. He was twisting from the waist as he said, "Billy! Gawddammit, he's gone!"

Not another word was said as the men recognized that indeed young Howe was not with them. Big Joe Fogarty blew out an exasperated breath.

McGregor stepped over and dropped to one knee beside Hugh Pepperdine. "You all right?" he asked.

Hugh looked up with a face made gray from exhaustion among other things, and lied, "Of course I'm all right. Just resting until some genius decides how we're goin' to get out of this mess."

The man on the porch dropped his smoke. They distinctly heard him grind it under a boot sole. That was the only sound as they scarcely breathed.

They still could not make him out, but when he turned toward the door he cleared his pipes and spat over the porch railing. They were beginning to relax as he approached the door, his obvious intention to go back into the house.

That old dog barked again, and this time as the barking trailed off, the dog growled deep in his throat. The man at the door stopped, turned very slowly back in the direction of the yard, stood a long time without moving, then moved to the steps.

The moment he was clear of the overhang they could see him, not in detail, but well enough to watch as he reached down to tug loose the tie-down thong over his holstered Colt.

Fogarty swore under his breath as the outlaw started

down the wide steps. It was a fair distance down to the
barn. As the man strolled in that direction, he would be
close enough to the west side of the yard to catch any
movement, no matter how furtive it was. It was too late
for them to retreat.

Roger Ames muttered something indistinguishable.
McGregor helped Hugh back to his feet and aligned the
long-barreled rifle so Hugh could lean on it. Hugh flintily
refused to acknowledge this solicitous interest by his old
friend. Like the others, he was watching the outlaw start
across the yard in starlight.

Fogarty had made up his mind. In a whisper so faint
those farthest from him could barely hear, he said, "The
minute he sees that empty tierack, he's going to raise a
yell. . . . I'm going to brace him after he's gone past."

It was not a plan, it was an act of desperation, and the
chances that the outlaw would not draw and fire were
slim. His kind reacted by instinct, not by reason;
otherwise they would fill a lot more graveyards than they
did.

Joe moved without a sound to the north corner of the
spring house, leaned a fraction to locate the outlaw, and
as the man passed into his line of sight, Joe rested his
right hand atop the saw handle of his side arm. The
outlaw was not walking fast, so it required a little time
for him to move ahead far enough so that Joe could step
out and call him from behind.

It never happened.

The outlaw stopped very suddenly, right hand near the
gun at his side. He could see the tierack with no horses
tethered to it. He hesitated for a long moment, possibly
speculating that the horses had freed themselves. But, of
course, while one or maybe two horses might have done
that, sure as hell seven hadn't.

He was like stone as possibilities passed through his

mind. Joe Fogarty had straightened up to step into the outlaw's path when an inflectionless voice spoke softly from among the sheds on the outlaw's left side.

"Don't make a sound. Don't move."

The outlaw obeyed. His right fingers were against the holstered six-gun on the right side. The voice was on his left.

"Shuck the gun! I'm goin' to blow your guts out past your backbone. *Drop it!*"

The men behind the spring house were transfixed. Roger Ames leaned to whisper in McGregor's ear. "That gawddamned kid!"

McGregor eased up beside Joe Fogarty, where he could see the outlaw, and raised his shotgun to belt-buckle height.

Billy spoke again. "You got two seconds to drop that gun."

The outlaw had arrived at his decision. He did not drop the gun. He drew it in a blur that was all but indistinguishable to the watchers, and fired three times so rapidly the explosions seemed to be one continuous roll of gun thunder. He had placed the area of the youth's voice. When he fired, he shot once to the left of the voice, once to the right of it and sent the third bullet squarely between the other two.

McGregor took one long sideward step to be well away from Marshal Fogarty, cocked the shotgun, and pulled the trigger. This time the blast was deafening. It was accompanied by a red muzzle flash. The outlaw, who had probably thought he was dealing with just one individual, never knew otherwise. At that range McGregor's lead slugs lifted the man completely off the ground and hurled him a good six feet before he fell, flopping like a beheaded chicken, riddled almost beyond belief.

The explosion had scarcely diminished when McGregor yelled at Billy Howe to get back over to the spring house, and called him a lot of names he would never forget.

McGregor broke his weapon, punched out the expended casing, and dug a replacement for it from a baggy pocket. He snapped the gun closed and glared as Billy came toward them from the direction of the barn. "I ought to blow your damned head off," McGregor said.

Joe Fogarty's big arm caught the youth by the shirt-front at the same moment the parlor light was doused at the main house and someone slammed the *tranca* down behind the front door.

Fogarty flung Billy away and faced around. Now everything had changed. The one element he had been relying on to offset their disadvantages had been destroyed. The men in the house knew they—someone anyway—were out there.

Roger Ames was peering around the south corner of the log wall in the direction of the house, silent and pensive. He was a top hand and a lifelong rangeman, and he had survived most of the perils of his calling by being circumspect. As he looked over his shoulder, where Hugh was leaning on a rifle, he said, "They're goin' to blow this spring house to kingdom come when they figure out we're behind it."

Hugh leaned aside the rifle and instinctively groped for chewing tobacco. There was none. He felt in every pocket, finally remembered using the last of it, and with a sigh retrieved the rifle to limp past Ames for a look at the house.

It could have been deserted for all he could hear or see. McGregor spoke behind him to Joe Fogarty. "They

got to have horses. We can't brace 'em with us outside
an' them inside. We'd ought to go back to the barn—
better shelter and they can't get no horses down there
with us watching."

Fogarty agreed and started toward the barn. He was
conscious of the cold and what it meant: Dawn was
coming. If he had not been sunk in gloom, he would
have seen Hugh raise his rifle at the southwest corner of
the spring house, take a hand rest against wood for the
barrel, and aim in the direction of the main house.

They were all moving away toward the distant barn,
when Hugh's squinty vigil was rewarded by what he
thought was shadowy movement. He fired at it. The
rifle's sound was distinctly different from the sound of a
carbine.

Fogarty swung, as did the others. Hugh was already
starting toward them when the return gunfire erupted. It
was not particularly dangerous to them, but they made
haste anyway. When they were inside the barn, Fogarty
asked Hugh what he had fired at. The harness maker
said, "Nothing. Maybe a shadow against the front of the
house. I just wanted them to know is all."

Evidently they "knew," because probing gunfire from
the house tore planks from the spring-house roof and
slivered the log walls.

Billy came up to say that the man they had left out
back trussed with his own belts was gone. That meant
there was a loose outlaw somewhere around. He could
not have reached the house; they would have seen him
trying to cross the yard. He was unarmed, but that was
little consolation.

McGregor put aside his scattergun, palmed his six-
gun, and went slowly up the loft pole, which was simply

a small tree trunk set into the earthen barn floor with slats spiked across it at short intervals.

The others waited. McGregor rattled wood before poking his head through the crawl hole, paused, made more noise, and finally stepped up one more rung and turned in all directions. It was darker up there than the inside of a boot. He saw nothing and was feeling with one foot for the next lower step, when a man said, "All right. I'll come down."

McGregor aimed in the direction of the voice, cocked his six-gun, and ordered the invisible man to toss away his gun. The man said, "I don't have no gun. You fellers took it."

McGregor guessed who the man was and remembered now seeing Billy pick up his discarded Colt. "You better not have," he warned the shadow that emerged from loose hay.

The others were around the base of the ladder watching McGregor scramble down. They waited briefly as a pair of legs appeared above, then moved back a little as the outlaw stepped gingerly from slat to slat all the way to the ground.

He had a lump on the side of his head and hair matted with blood. Visibility was not good enough for them to see that his eyes were bloodshot, or that his face was gray from pain.

They took him to the rear barn opening and told him to lie flat to be searched. He obeyed as he had done once before when told to get belly-down, but this time he was too demoralized to attempt anything.

CHAPTER THIRTEEN

Hugh's Recollection

His name was Carl Whitten, he told them, and he was very thirsty. There were canteens on the horses they had left out yonder and they were going to stay out there. Joe Fogarty found a little wooden horseshoe keg and kicked it toward the man, who sank down upon it gratefully. He did not feel good or look good. Where McGregor had struck him on the side of the head there was a large swelling. It was discolored, but in barn gloom that was not noticeable.

Joe sent Billy and Roger Ames to watch the front of the house, leaned on a saddle pole eyeing Carl Whitten, and said, "How many are in the house?"

Whitten's watering eyes made him lustily blow his nose before replying. "Five now. I seen one of you blow Cal Forrester out of his boots a while back. Without Cal an' me there is five."

There were a lot of questions to be asked, but most of them could wait. Fogarty asked the prisoner who the head outlaw was and got back an answer that made the men in the barn stare at him.

"Hiram Simpson. He says he's the nephew to President Grant. You ever heard of Hy Simpson?"

Fogarty shook his head. "No."

Before Whitten could be asked another question, Billy Howe said, "What happened when you fellers rode in? Did my paw or grandpaw or the old Mex get hurt?"

Whitten lustily blew his nose for the second time. "No. It was like catchin' fish in a rain barrel. They was in the barn, didn't see us coming nor hear us. They had a rawboned chestnut colt snubbed in there. They was fixing to shoe him, but he had other ideas. We just walked in from both ends and threw down on 'em." Whitten looked briefly painless as he recalled that fortuitous event. Then he raised a stiff handkerchief to his watering eyes.

When he spoke again it was after a period of silence among the men staring at him. He said, "Who'n hell are you? Where'd you come from?"

Fogarty told him. He also asked the name of the man who had killed the hostler up in Sheridan, and Whitten answered without hesitation. "Jack Porter. He's a Canadian. He joined us up yonder in Montana. Been with us all the time, right down to this damned place. He's in the house over yonder."

"Who was the preacher who held the prayer meeting up at Sheridan?" Hugh asked, and got back another direct reply.

"Parson Reynolds. Pretty good at it, ain't he?" Whitten dabbed at his eyes again. "Ain't there some water in here?"

No one answered. Across the yard a watery shade of gray was spreading. It presaged dawn. As visibility in the barn improved, the men could see their prisoner's swollen, discolored injury. They could also see one another. There was not a man in the barn who did not look like something left behind after a massacre. They were filthy, unshaven, red-eyed, and tucked up.

Roger Ames turned from up front and said, "You fellers hungry? Well, they're frying meat and spuds over there."

That did not make Fogarty's men feel any better. The prisoner fished in a pocket, bit a corner off a frayed plug, and before he could return it to his pocket, Hugh Pepperdine snatched it from him, gnawed some off, and pocketed the plug without even saying thank you.

McGregor had a question for Carl Whitten. "How much money you fellers get from all those banks you robbed?"

Whitten looked balefully at the gunsmith. "I'm dryin' up from thirst, and you want to talk about money."

McGregor raised his shotgun belly-high and pointed it.

Whitten seemed mesmerized by the ugly twin barrels. "According to Hy Simpson, we got about thirty-five thousand dollars." The outlaw's eyes raised slowly. "When we get to Messico, each of us can live for a long time on his share. You got any idea how much money thirty-five thousand dollars is?"

Instead of an answer, Whitten got a curse from McGregor, then a cold statement. "You're never going to reach Messico. Neither are your friends, an' if I had my way about it, I'd burn that house to the ground with them inside it."

Billy swung his head toward the gunsmith. If he'd had in mind speaking, the opportunity was preempted by Ames, who was still up front watching the house. "There's movement behind the front window. Couldn't see it before. Maybe we could thin them out a little more."

Fogarty went up there as McGregor and Billy Howe went to work lashing Carl Whitten's hands behind his back, using rope this time, then pushed him back down on the horseshoe keg as they joined the others up front peeking in the direction of the main house.

The aroma of cooking food was tantalizing, but the smell of boiling coffee made Hugh groan aloud. They had not eaten since the evening before, and they hadn't been able to fill up then. Hugh said, "Right this minute I'd start eatin' from the rear end of a rattlesnake if someone was holdin' its head."

A deep, resonant voice abruptly came down through the cold predawn as far, and farther, than the barn. Whoever the speaker was, and the listeners assumed he would be the man named Simpson, leader of the outlaw band, his words as well as his voice showed no anxiety. What he said was probably the reason.

"We got a trade for you fellers down at the barn. We got three hostages in here. Most likely you wouldn't want to see them shoved out onto the porch, where we'd shoot them, so all you got to do is saddle up them horses we had ready last night, walk out a half mile or so without your guns, and we'll leave 'em behind."

Obviously, the forted-up outlaws had held an earlier discussion. Their proposal did not sound spontaneous. Hugh said, "Ever since we started after 'em I've wondered about them mattresses they put in front of the bank vaults. Right now I'm beginnin' to suspect that feller over yonder is a hell of a long way from being stupid."

No one took this up. Roger Ames was watching young Billy like a hawk. Billy's face was white. He ignored his uncle to face Joe Fogarty when he said, "Burn the house . . . With paw an' grandpaw an' old Carlos inside it?"

The big lawman's answer was indicative of his thoughts. "Naw. If we don't come up with something else, we'll give them the horses."

McGregor looked past out into the dawn-breaking east, where a sky as flawless as pale silk spread in all directions. He said nothing, but his expression was bleak. He had not come this far, gone through all the suffering it had taken to corner the outlaws, to present them with the means of making their final race down over the line into Mexico.

The deep voice called out again. "Take your time, boys. We ain't finished breakfast anyway."

Hugh rolled his eyes while muttering to himself. He envisioned a mounded platter of fried meat, maybe feather-light baking-powder biscuits, spuds fried golden brown, and coffee strong enough to float a horseshoe.

Joe Fogarty walked back away from the front opening to lean on the saddle pole. Billy broke into his thoughts with a half question. "You fellers can't want those bastards that bad. You can't figure the money is more important than what the man said they do."

Pepperdine was jettisoning his cud and gazing at their captive. He did not take his eyes off the prisoner when he replied to the youth. "Naw. Just set back a little and leave us figure for a minute or two, Billy."

He then addressed Marshal Fogarty. "Right this minute I'd trade my soul for a platter of biscuits slathered with gravy and a cup of that coffee." He paused. "Let me tell you somethin' I saw done one time about thirty years ago when some Mex *bandoleros* came charging up over the line to raise hell and steal horses. The army got between them an' the border, a big mob of stockmen got behind them in the other direction." Hugh had everyone's attention and was enjoying it, despite his assorted aches. "Now then, those Messicans had three ranch women they was takin' back down into Messico with them. When they saw the army in front with more armed men than they could shake a stick at, an' darn near as many mad-as-hornets stockmen fannin' out in back of them, why they just naturally stopped, hid in the rocks, tied a white rag on a pole, and made about the same proposition those fellers at the house just made: They'd abandon the stolen horses and set the three ladies free if the ranchers and soldiers would let them escape back down into Messico."

Hugh paused. There was not a sound in the barn, or in the yard either. Even the outlaw sitting on the little wooden keg was watching him. He smiled. "That's the first time I ever heard somethin' called a Messican standoff."

McGregor was beginning to look impatient. "You should have been a preacher," he growled. "Get to the point, Hugh."

"I'm gettin' to the point. Just relax, James. . . . Well now, there was a big confab between the stockmen an' the soldiers. One old soldier, I forget his name but he was burnt brown and wrinkled like a prune, he come up with a solution. So they agreed to the deal, but only providin' the Messicans came out of the rocks for a palaver, which they did, and while they was all sittin' on the ground, that soldier an' a cowboy slunk around into the rocks and cut the cinches to every one of their saddled horses, leaving just two strands."

Hugh stopped speaking and looked around, waiting. McGregor gazed steadily at his old friend for a long time. The others looked elsewhere, at one another, at the prisoner, even out into the sun-lighted cool yard. McGregor said, "You never told me that story before, Hugh."

Pepperdine was skiving off a cud from the plug he'd taken from their captive when he answered. "You 'n' I never been together in a fix like this before."

Joe Fogarty straightened up off the saddle pole to step back a little and reach for one of the traditional cinches that was latigoed to a saddle that had been removed from one of those seven horses. It consisted of twenty-one strands of twisted horsehair. He held it, turned it over, looked up a little skeptically, and said, "You think we ought to try it?"

They nodded, even McGregor, who was still regarding his old friend dourly.

Fogarty dropped the cinch. "Show 'em," he told Hugh, and paced back to the front barn doorway, pulled in a breath, and called in the direction of the main house. "Simpson?"

A belated reply came. "Yeah. How'd you know my name?"

"We got a man named Whitten down here with us. Simpson, you bring those hostages with you."

The deep voice boomed right back. "Agreed. You tie the horses to the rack and walk out a half mile. We'll be lookin' for guns. Leave 'em all in the barn. Don't try anything or we'll kill these old men and the Mexican. . . . Who are you?"

"Town Marshal Fogarty from Sheridan."

"How many men with you?"

McGregor reached quickly and squeezed the lawman's arm, shaking his head. "Tell him four men."

That was the number Joe called back. He also

said, "There are more riders coming. They'd ought to maybe be here within the next two or three hours."

Simpson's reply was a drawl. "Let 'em come, Marshal. Now, you get them horses rigged out and put out front. We'll be watchin' like hawks. One wrong move and you're goin' to have three dead men on your hands."

Joe stepped back and faced around. The prisoner said, "You lied to him. Let me tell you somethin' about the fellers over there. Every damned one of 'em is a dead shot. Tryin' to be clever is goin' to get you killed."

Roger Ames spoke softly to the captive. "We got you, an' there's that one lyin' out yonder. None of us been killed yet."

Whitten glowered and said no more.

Hugh's sore knee did not seem to be bothering him very much now as he showed the others how to cut cinch strands where the girth came up directly beneath the horse and how to conceal the severed strands by tying them together so that they would not hang loose and show. He even seemed to have forgotten his hunger and his swollen face. Once he looked over where the dour McGregor was working, and winked. McGregor wagged his head. "If this works, I'll buy you a new hat," he muttered.

"You already owe me one," Pepperdine retorted. "I don't need two hats. If it works, you can stand me to drinks at Rusty's saloon for a week."

Ames did not allow his nephew out of his sight, which was probably a good thing because ever since that talk about burning the ranch house with his relatives inside, Billy had been both quiet and agitated.

As they worked, Ames asked if there really was someone coming from up north. Joe had no doubt but that riders from up north were out there somewhere. Whether they would find this ranch, or tracks leading to it, was something he did not dwell upon. His comment was simply that after two towns had been raided and a man had been murdered in one of them, it wasn't likely that there weren't riders on the way.

They finished with the cinches. McGregor inspected each one as Billy and his uncle went after the horses. Hugh watched the gunsmith and finally said, "They're all right. All we got to do is be real careful when we saddle up the mounts. Two strands will hold a saddle long enough for a man to swing up. That's all we want, what with you hidin' back here in the barn with that shotgun. If you let 'em all get astride then fire both barrels at the same time, the damned commotion will set every horse out there to either runnin' with a bit in his teeth or bucking like he never cut loose before."

McGregor raised up, looking aggravated. "Both barrels at the same time? You got any idea what'll happen if I do that?"

Hugh was unperturbed. "Yeah. The recoil will knock you on your butt. Well, you been usin' it for everythin' else lately, on horseback through rocks and whatnot. One more bump hadn't ought to make much difference."

The prisoner laughed, which startled everyone. He eyed Pepperdine with respect. "For an old gaffer, I got to hand it to you. You're a tough old goat. You can't fight worth a damn, but you're tough."

Hugh hauled straight up. "Can't fight worth a damn? If James hadn't hauled you off me, I'd have broke half the bones in your miserable carcass."

Whitten looked bemused and did not argue. They were ready to lead the saddle animals out to the rack. As they were doing this, he called to Fogarty. "Hey, lawman, Hy's no fool. He's goin' to figure out you're up to something. He'll shoot them prisoners at the drop of a hat, then you."

Joe kept his back to the outlaw and led a horse toward the barn doorway.

CHAPTER FOURTEEN

Problems

It was not hot out yet but it was going to be. Inside the barn, it was both cool and shadowy. Fogarty and Pepperdine led two horses outside and tied them there. Before returning for the next two horses, they glanced at the house across saddle seats.

Joe led the last animal out. It was a pig-eyed sorrel who looked as if both his ears came out the same hole. He was rawboned and rangy with big feet. When Joe got back to the protection of the barn, Roger Ames nodded toward the tierack. "It don't take much to make that sorrel bust in two."

Later, when Roger and Billy came inside from out back carrying canteens, the captive outlaw watched those canteens go past as if they were solid gold.

Everyone had a drink, the prisoner last. Marshal Fogarty turned to leave the barn again. When he was among the tethered horses, he called toward the house. "Simpson? Did you count 'em? Five horses."

"Make it six," came back the shout. "We're goin' to

take Whitten with us. Rig out another one and hurry up about it."

Fogarty returned to the barn, where Ames was already hoisting a saddle onto the back of a dappled horse. Whitten watched the saddling with a troubled gaze. He finally said, "Tell you what: I'd as soon not go out there."

Hugh nodded. "I don't blame you. But your boss said for you to go, and that's that."

Whitten was eyeing McGregor and his double-barreled scattergun, when he shook his head. "Naw. Tell 'em I'm hurt too bad to move. Tell 'em I can't set a saddle."

Roger Ames finished saddling the horse and faced Carl Whitten. "Thought you was plumb certain this wouldn't come off. Now you're scairt it will, and you'll be caught in the middle."

The outlaw offered no denial. "Hell yes. Whether it works or not, I'll be a target atop a horse with a cinch that won't hold together. And me with no weapon. You think I'm crazy?"

Hugh leaned with his long-barreled rifle and poked the outlaw in the kidneys from in back. Whitten shot up off the horseshoe keg, flinching. He controlled the pain as he said, "Marshal, you take me out there where I'm most likely goin' to get killed anyway, an' I'm goin' to yell to Hy the minute he comes out of the house that it's a trick."

Simpson's booming voice interrupted. "Hey, Marshal, where's that sixth horse?"

Joe returned to the sunlight. "He's ready."

Billy led him out and looped the reins. He glared in the direction of the house for a long moment before trudging back where it was cool.

Fogarty, with his back to the men in the barn, watched the house. Behind him the prisoner was beginning to sweat. He knew what lay ahead. When his remarks went unanswered, he asked for a canteen. Roger Ames handed him one, and he seemed to drink for an unusually long time before stoppering the container and handing it back. He looked Ames in the eye and said, "You're goin' to have to drag me out there."

The cowboy neither moved nor spoke. He eyed the outlaw with strong distaste and turned when the deep voice bellowed from the house again.

"Now then, walk out into the yard, all of you, and head north. No guns. If we see a gun, you're goin' to wish to hell you never tried it."

Fogarty yelled back. "Yeah. When we see you on the porch with the hostages."

There was a moment of quiet before Simpson yelled again. "Oh, no. Not with you still armed and in the barn. Leave the weapons behind and start walking. *Now!*"

James McGregor looked at his old friend. "Lean the rifle aside, Hugh. He's not a fool. If you walk a half mile out, even if you conceal a six-gun you couldn't be accurate with it at that distance."

Fogarty walked back down to where they were talking and nodded at Hugh. "Stick a pistol in the front of your britches but leave the rifle in here. All of you—hide the six-guns. Do it real good because he's goin' to suspect something."

They did as McGregor and Fogarty had suggested, and hid their handguns. As they were doing so, Whitten said, "You darned fools. Leave the six-guns. If he even suspicions you got 'em, they're all goin' to open up on you from in back. Besides, like the man said, six-guns aren't no good at a half mile. Why risk it?"

Roger Ames cast a scathing look upon the injured outlaw. He probably was not going to speak, but Hugh Pepperdine did something that scotched even the possibility of further argument. He hit Whitten over the head with his pistol barrel. As Whitten dropped, Hugh addressed Marshal Fogarty. "Leave him here for them to find. He's not goin' to yell no warning now, and he's not goin' to come around anytime soon either."

Fogarty scowled at Hugh, but since their prisoner was already unconscious he ignored the sprawled man and jerked his head. "Let's go."

Fogarty turned up near the barn opening to look at McGregor. The gunsmith looked flintily back and gestured. "Go on. He's not goin' to wait forever and neither am I."

Hugh limped past his friend and paused. McGregor treated him the same way. "Just get on out of here."

"Be careful, James."

McGregor's pale gaze did not waver. "I'll be careful. It's you fellers who'll be out in the open when all hell breaks loose. I'll have rifles and my handgun in here."

Fogarty jerked his head. They trooped out of the barn into blazing sunlight like squaw Indians, one behind the other. Even Billy did not look around. When they had reached the north edge of the yard, Fogarty turned to yell toward the house. It was not necessary. The outlaws were easing out onto the long porch pushing ahead three men whose arms were bound behind them.

Fogarty continued to walk. He felt bitter. If the renegades had not caught those three hostages . . . But they had.

Ames muttered quietly. "Slow down, Marshal. If we're still within runnin' distance of the trees on the west side when McGregor spooks the horses we can reach cover."

But the outlaws did not move out of the overhang shade. They were clearly waiting for the walking men to get farther away before heading for the tierack.

Each of them looked back a time or two. Hugh made a correct guess about the large, thick man standing to the right of the prisoners on the porch. "That'll be Simpson."

Billy spoke for the first time in a long while. "He ain't so clever. If he was, he'd know there was one more man around somewhere."

Billy's uncle turned irritably. "How would he know?"

Billy did not reply.

It was still early morning, but the heat was palpable. By midafternoon it was going to be hot enough to fry eggs on a rock.

Fogarty had sighted on a scattering of bone-gray boulders, which was the place he expected to halt. Sweat ran under his shirt. He glanced to one side where Hugh was hiking along, not limping. The harness maker met his gaze with a thin smile. "It stopped botherin' me after a hundred yards."

Fogarty nodded approval. "My paw used to say the best medicine for somethin' like that was exercise. I wish to hell I hadn't listened to James. They can have their stolen money and the horses."

Hugh spat amber, ran a filthy cuff across his lower face, and replied curtly. "You know James. Nobody ever shook an idea out of his head once it got in there."

Billy spoke quickly in a high voice. "They're standin' behind the tierack watching us."

Hugh and Joe Fogarty glanced back. The outlaws were indeed watching from behind the tethered horses. They probably wanted to make certain Fogarty and his companions were well out of handgun range before they unlooped the reins and got astride.

Roger Ames lifted his hat, mopped sweat, dropped the hat back down, and started walking again. "We're too far," he said. "We'll never be able to get back in time to help McGregor when he needs us."

Neither of the men who knew McGregor well commented. But Billy had something to say. "Sure as hell there's going to be shooting. My paw's goin' to be standing there like a wooden Indian."

Nobody commented about that either. They were beyond the point of speculating. Whatever was going to happen was simply going to happen. But Joe Fogarty was slowing, and the others followed his example. They were still a fair distance from the bone-gray rocks. Joe's earlier statement about allowing the renegades to flee with their stolen money had been one of those remarks a dispirited man made. It did not really reflect his deep-down feeling.

He felt for the handle of the Colt in the front of his britches as he halted to look back. Around him the others also turned, but Joe was the only one with his hand on a gun stock.

That big, thick outlaw was easy to distinguish among his companions. He stood a moment squinting out where his enemies had stopped, then probably said something, because each man eased in on the left side of a tethered horse. One man backed a horse clear and peered down inside the barn, led his animal to the front opening, and called back to his companions.

It required no particular gift to guess that he had seen the unconscious outlaw down in the barn. The leader looked over his shoulder and said something that made the outlaw in front of the barn turn to mount his horse. It was clear to the distant watchers that Simpson meant to abandon Whitten, leaving him lying in the barn.

Not a man out there northward of the yard in blazing sunlight seemed to be breathing. The outlaws swung up behind the large man, who pointed his horse southward, riding at a walk on an angling course to avoid the main house, when an explosion that sounded like ten sticks of dynamite detonating in unison made the heavy air quiver as far out as Fogarty and his companions.

There was one horse still at the tierack. He hurled back, broke the reins, and charged directly into the melee of bucking animals, screaming outlaws, and rising dust.

Two saddles went up into the air with their passengers still toed into the stirrups. Another cinch broke when an outlaw savagely yanked back to keep his animal from getting its head down to buck. The horse went straight up and over backward. Both saddle and rider were flung sideways. If that cinch had not broken when it had, there was a very good chance the outlaw would have been killed by a saddle horn through his brisket. It happened often with up-and-over horses.

The big man was fighting a stud-necked bay horse who had bogged his head the moment the explosion erupted behind him. As strong as the large man was, he could not get the horse's head up. He made a good ride as long as it lasted. His animal knew about bucking. He had his head between his knees. Every time he hit the ground he bawled.

Then the cinch broke.

Simpson had been leaning back, feet thrust forward. When the saddle broke free, the horse bucked out from under him, leaving him to turn an almost complete somersault, still clinging to the saddle.

Hugh yelled. "Let's go!" He led the run back toward the yard. After a few yards his leg started hurting again.

The others passed him, but old Hugh gritted his teeth, yanked out his six-gun, and continued to run.

The runners were still half the distance from the yard when one of the outlaws called to another man who had risen out of the dust to yell. Hugh heard the words perfectly.

"In the barn! He's in the barn!"

Hugh locked his jaw and forced himself to run faster as the two rumpled, hatless outlaws moved cat-footedly toward either side of the barn opening, handguns up and ready.

That was when the second deafening explosion sent echoes in all directions for miles.

Those two outlaws flung themselves against the front of the barn and stayed there.

Their companions were picking themselves up, all but the bearded man who had pretended to be a preacher up at Sheridan. He had almost completed a cartwheel with the saddle still between his legs. He had landed with his head bent forward so that the full force of the fall came on his neck.

He was still lying out there with both arms close to his body, one leg jackknifed over the other leg, the saddle wrong side up about five feet away.

There was no sign of the hostages whose arms had been tied behind their backs. It seemed unlikely that they would have rushed into the safety of the barn after someone in there had fired both barrels of a shotgun. There were other places among nearby outbuildings where they could take shelter.

There were four live outlaws on foot. Two were ignoring everything but loose saddle horses. Their friends were stuck along the front of the barn as still as statues. McGregor's second blast had nearly deafened them; it had certainly frightened them.

Hugh was dropping back with sweat running under his clothes like rainwater. Billy was the fleetest. He reached the edge of the yard and without stopping to aim, fired three shots at the men in front of the barn.

One of them turned and fired back, shooting from the hip in what should have been a waste of lead, except that this man never shot any other way.

Billy went over backward as though struck squarely by an invisible fist. His uncle stopped close by, sank to one knee, and fired at the outlaw. So did Fogarty and Hugh, but Hugh was gasping like a fish out of water. His bullet struck the logs eighteen inches above his target.

Ames and Fogarty must have come close. The outlaw jumped, then sprinted to the barn opening and sprang inside. His companion did the same, and Hugh howled a wild curse. McGregor and his shotgun were no match for two gunfighters. They may not even have been the match for one gunfighter.

Hugh started running as hard as he could. Breath burst past his lips, his leg threatened to crumple under him, and the side of his face where Whitten had struck him throbbed fiercely.

CHAPTER FIFTEEN

The Diminishing Opposition

One outlaw had caught a saddleless horse and was trying to mount bareback, but the horse had been badly frightened by the noise and dust and was dragging him by the reins.

The other man who'd been trying to catch a horse gave it up. The outlaw saw the men running back from the north. He saw Billy fire and go down when someone fired back. He looked quickly around, then ran in the direction of the main house.

No one heeded him.

Hugh came up to the front of the barn and leaned there to favor his leg and suck air. He hadn't run that hard in fifteen years. There were agitated horses in several directions, all without saddles. The outlaw who had been doggedly hanging on to the reins finally gave up and released one. The loose horse turned and fled toward the rear of the barn.

Hugh called to the man to shove both arms over his head. It was possible the outlaw did not hear him. He looked around the yard, found himself entirely alone, and flung one wild shot in the direction of the barn as he whirled and raced toward the main house.

Hugh settled his handgun to track the man with. Someone fired from behind the barn somewhere and the running man went end over end and fetched up scuffling in the dust.

Joe Fogarty sent Ames to watch the front of the barn with Hugh while he went around in back. Gradually, the racket and frantic movement ceased. The dust settled. What should have been a successful flight of outlaws had turned into something altogether different. There were two left inside the barn, one man in the main house. Otherwise, there was no one in sight who would be able to resist Fogarty's men from Sheridan.

As silence gradually returned, Roger Ames came up behind the Sheridan harness maker and leaned to whisper. "Any sound of 'em down in there?"

Hugh shook his head without speaking. There should have been sound; there should have been a gunfight in there when McGregor saw the outlaws running toward his barn.

Fogarty called from out back for the outlaws to pitch out their weapons. His answer was a six-gun blast that peeled a long sliver from one of the doorway baulks.

Hugh got flat down, put his hat aside, and eased foward until he could see the barn's interior with one eye. There was no one in sight. He waited for movement and saw none, so he pushed backward until he could stand up. Ames waited until Hugh had shaken off most of the dust. "Didn't see anything?"

Hugh shook his head. "Not a thing."

"Then McGregor is hiding somewhere an' they haven't found him."

Hugh made no comment about this. Sooner or later

those gunfighters were going to either see or hear
McGregor, and when they did they'd kill him.

Fogarty called out again. "We can keep you in there
until winter. It's up to you." What Joe was worrying
about was that if those men caught McGregor, they'd
have something to trade for their freedom. Another
damned hostage situation.

Time passed, heat built up, and that dead man who'd
been blown apart by McGregor's shotgun much earlier
was beginning to look like he'd need to be either put in a
cool place or buried.

There was another man farther out, much larger. He
had not moved since landing with his neck bent. He, too,
would have to be dragged out of direct sunlight soon.

The man who had run for the house and had been shot
before he got there was dragging himself toward the
porch. No one heeded him.

Heat beat against the front of the barn. Hugh mopped
sweat and told Roger Ames that sure as hell those holed-
up renegades in the barn were going to lie still until
nightfall. He said Ames should go look after young Billy
Howe. The rangeman reset his hat to keep sun from his
eyes before replying. "He'll be all right. Last Christmas
his paw gave him a big, heavy pocket watch. That there
thing was Billy's greatest treasure. The bullet hit it,
busting it all to hell. I put Billy over on the north side of
the barn to rest a spell. He's sore and bruised, but he'll be
fine."

The outlaw holed up in the main house changed the
situation by firing at the front of the barn where Ames
and Pepperdine were. He came close enough to make
both men jump, duck down, and dash frantically around
the northward corner.

Neither of them fired back, so the silence returned,

thick with oppressive heat. Ames left Hugh to seek
Marshal Fogarty. The north side of the barn was cool
compared with the front. Hugh glanced along the wall,
saw Billy sitting there, and went down to him to ask if he
had any idea where his paw and the other captives were.
Billy looked up with a flushed face. "Probably in the
bunkhouse."

Hugh eyed the youth. Except for red-rimmed eyes and
a high flush from the heat, he seemed to be in fair shape.
Hugh glanced upward then downward. "Tell you what I
got in mind," he murmured to the youth. "If you'll lend
a hand, I think I can go up that pulley rope and get into
the loft."

Billy's expression changed as he, too, eyed the small
loft doorway overhead. After a time of thought he got to
his feet. "Naw. You lend me a hand and I'll go up there.
That's mighty hard work pullin' yourself up the rope,
even with someone down here pulling on the slack end of
the block and tackle."

Pepperdine yielded even though his masculine sen-
sitivity had been wounded. He gazed at the younger
man. Billy was wiry and strong, but most of all in his
favor, he was young. Hugh sighed to himself, then
limped over to catch hold of the dangling rope and walk
back with it.

Billy raised both arms and flinched. Hugh's brow
furrowed. "You better not try it, being hurt and all. We'd
be in a hell of a fix if you was halfway up there an' had to
drop down. You could bust a leg."

Billy was shaking his head long before the harness
maker finished speaking. "It's just a bruise. It won't
bother my arm for climbing."

Hugh fashioned several hand-hold knots at intervals.
Billy grasped the lower one, turned his head so that

Hugh could not see his face, and strained upward. Hugh leaned all his weight upon the slack rope.

It was hard work. Hugh thought of a number of rueful remarks but said none of them. He instead strained on the rope as Billy climbed higher, and squinted at the little loft door. If Billy swung too close in his ascent and scraped along the upper woodwork, anyone inside the loft would hear him, guess what was in progress, and probably greet Billy with the snout of a gun in his face.

Out back Joe Fogarty was calling to the forted-up outlaws in the barn again. In the yard, two of the saddleless horses were still hanging around, bridled and with reins dragging. The heat was still strong. Roger Ames came around from the rear of the barn and halted in his tracks with a slack jaw as he saw his nephew suspended by a rope near the little loft door overhead. Hugh was panting. "Lend a hand. That boy's heavier'n he looks," he whispered.

Ames added his weight on the rope. Billy covered the final few feet and hung almost directly below the wooden tackle blocks suspended from a massive log ridgepole that extended beyond the barn wall by about three feet. He could lean and open the door.

The men on the ground watched, scarcely breathing, as Billy lifted out his waistband revolver, clutched it in the same hand he was holding the rope with, and leaned to grasp the loft door. He tried to aim the gun as he swung the door outward. If there had been someone hostile behind the little door, Billy probably wouldn't have hit him even at close range because of his grip on the rope and the gun at the same time.

But there was no one waiting for him. He pulled himself as close as he could get with his free hand, shoved the gun into his britches, reached out with both hands, kicked free of the rope, and threw himself inside into the hay.

His uncle released the rope and raised a filthy sleeve to mop off sweat with. "Whose damned idea was that? Them outlaws could be burrowed in the hay waiting for him."

Hugh did not say whose idea it had been. He answered the second half of Ames's objection. "If they was up there, you'd have heard gunfire by now."

They waited. There was not a sound. The silence was so complete they could hear a horse slopping water after he had drunk his fill out back where there was an old stone trough.

Hugh nudged the cowboy. "Go tell Joe to keep talkin' to those bastards in the barn. Keep their attention on him."

Ames eyed Pepperdine suspiciously. "Why? Now what you got in mind?"

Hugh smiled; his sweat-greasy, lumpy, unshaven face was gargoylelike. "Just simply keepin' their mind on the rear doorway. That's all."

Ames was not satisfied with that explanation but turned to hike back around to the rear of the barn where Marshal Fogarty was keeping a vigil.

The moment Ames was out of sight Hugh sidled back up to the northeast corner of the barn and leaned out slowly until he could see the main house and that injured outlaw who had left squiggly snake tracks from where he had been hit to the wide, low stairs leading up onto the porch. The outlaw was up there, but flat down and unmoving. He had either lost consciousness or was dead.

Hugh waited a long time. He studied the shadows and the places where sunlight reached beneath the overhanging roof. What he had in mind was slipping along the front of the barn to the doorway, and while Joe Fogarty was holding the attention of the besieged outlaws, to whip around into the barn and duck for cover.

But he could do none of this as long as there was someone over in the main house with a clear view of the barn.

Fogarty's alternate threats and promises began again. Hugh hoped to see a shadow move over at the main house. All he saw was an old dog, troubled by arthritis, get up off a bed of croaker sacks and go awkwardly over to the motionless outlaw and sniff.

Hugh looked for a rock, found one, exposed himself for five seconds as he wound up and hurled the stone. It did not reach the roof but it rattled down the porch overhang. The arthritic old dog gave a little start, but that was the only reaction.

Hugh was disappointed but not surprised; that was the oldest ruse in the world. He considered putting a couple of shots into the house. That would almost certainly get a violent reaction. He did not have the opportunity to do it.

Two explosions inside the barn, one loud, one deafening, shattered the silence, sending echoes in all directions for a considerable distance.

Hugh recovered from his surprise. The louder blast had been from a shotgun. The other sound had been made by a handgun. He waited; at fairly close range it was easier to miss with a revolver than it was with a scattergun.

Joe Fogarty yelled from out back. "McGregor? You all right?"

McGregor did not reply; a stranger did, his voice almost shrill. "I quit! You hear me? I'm goin' to pitch my gun out back."

Hugh leaned to squint in the direction of the house. There was no indication that the man over there was reacting to the ruckus in the barn. It slowly dawned on Hugh that with just about everyone else accounted for, that had to be Simpson at the house.

Fogarty spoke loudly to someone out behind the barn. If the man he had addressed responded, Hugh could not make it out because two other voices broke across the lawman's words. Hugh recognized them both. One voice belonged to James McGregor. The other one was Billy Howe's voice, slightly shrill with excitement as Hugh had heard it at other times.

He leaned back, rested his sore leg briefly, then started back around the log wall toward the shady area behind the barn.

Fogarty was shoving a short, wiry man against the log wall with one hand and pushing a cocked pistol into his back with the other hand. As Hugh approached, the outlaw turned his head. Hugh thought that if ever a man resembled a weasel, that son of a bitch sure did, with his pointy face and pinched-together eyes. Hugh abruptly stopped dead still as two men appeared in the shaded rear barn doorway. He loosened at the sight of a shotgun in the hands of a dour-looking man his own age and smiled. "What'd you shoot at, James?"

The gunsmith swung a smoldering gaze from the outlaw spread-eagled against the log wall to the harness maker. "Dang near shot this kid," he growled. "When he come through that little door, I was expecting someone else."

Billy looked sideways at the older man. He had his six-gun shoved back into the front of his britches. He had chaff and stalks of bleached hay adhering to his clothing.

When Hugh came closer, Billy answered the question McGregor had ignored.

"There was two of 'em. One of 'em heard something in the loft. He was comin' toward the loft ladder when that one the marshal's got hold of told him to stand clear of the ladder an' he'd fire up through the floor. We could see the first one, the feller near the ladder. Mr. McGregor cocked his shotgun, nodded to me, an' we both fired at the one we could see. The other one give up."

Roger Ames came along from south of the barn. He was in no hurry, but his stride was purposeful. When he came up as Marshal Fogarty was stepping back from searching their captive, he said, "If Whitten's alive in the barn, counting this scrawny one we got three survivors."

Hugh asked about the one who had dragged himself to the porch and Ames replied with one word. "Dead."

"And the one in the house?"

Roger reached inside his shirt to vigorously scratch as he answered. "I tallied 'em, and the one I can't account for is that big feller, Simpson."

"You scouted up the house, Mr. Ames?"

"Well, yes. But when I figured it up and come up short on that big feller, why then he had to be in the house, so I come back."

Hugh wryly nodded his head. "Don't blame you," he murmured.

Billy approached his uncle. "Where's paw?"

Ames jerked his head. "Forted up in the bunkhouse. I told him it was over, but he wouldn't come out. Come along, maybe he'll listen to you."

Hugh watched them depart, thinking that it wasn't over, and if they weren't careful they'd find out the hard way that it wasn't.

Joe took their prisoner into the cool barn, shoved him toward a horseshoe keg, and watched Pepperdine and McGregor approach Carl Whitten, who did not appear to have moved at all after being struck over the head.

They got the injured man propped in front of a horse stall, got hatfuls of water from the trough out back, and soaked him. He flopped and made choking sounds but did not completely recover until after a man's scream from somewhere outside distracted everyone.

It was an incoherent outcry followed by two rapid gunshots.

The men in the barn scattered, some toward the front, at least two of them, the harness maker and the gunsmith, toward the back of the barn.

There was one more gunshot. Hugh looked darkly at McGregor. "Them damned fools," he said, and led off toward the south corner of the big old log structure.

McGregor did not stay behind his friend; he moved clear of him on his right, leaned far around, stiffened, and said, "Gawddam, he's got a horse!"

Hugh stepped away from protective logs, gun rising. There were two men on the ground in front of the bunkhouse. Hugh recognized them both, Billy Howe and his uncle.

Simpson was thunderously cursing at a terrified horse he was trying to control by the reins. He saw McGregor step into sight from behind the barn, twisted, and fired. The bullet came close enough to make McGregor flinch.

Hugh was raising his pistol when around in front of the barn two men fired, one with a handgun, which made a loud noise, and one with a Winchester, which made a more waspish report.

The horse hurled himself backward, broke free, and nearly upset Simpson as he did so. The animal wheeled and fled. Simpson was down on one knee when he fired three times in the direction of the barn front, hurled the gun away, and yanked a second one from his waistband.

Hugh took three wide steps, got clear of the barn, yelled "Hey, you son of a bitch!" and methodically aimed low and emptied his weapon. Simpson fired twice, once close enough for Hugh to feel a rush of air, the second time into the ground four feet in front of himself as his body was curling forward. He was dead before reaching the ground. His heavy body collapsed slowly, almost tiredly.

CHAPTER SIXTEEN

Toward Sundown

Billy had been hit by Hy Simpson's first bullet. The wound was through the fleshy part of his upper left leg. It bled profusely until his father and the Mexican, who had not left the bunkhouse when the firing started, tied it off.

Simpson's second gunshot had put Roger Ames down with a notched ear and a long red raker across the side of his head. Everything would eventually heal and return to normal except for the tip of Roger's ear, which was completely gone.

They were carried to the main house, which was a shambles. Billy's father and grandfather were medium-sized, work-roughened men. The Mexican was not young either, but he showed it less than the other two. The story they told was about as Carl Whitten had said; they had been caught off guard and none of them was armed, which Joe Fogarty said dryly was just as well.

Hugh walked back from gazing at Hy Simpson, looked at the Howes, and bluntly asked about food. The older Howe and the Mexican returned to the house. Billy and his father dragged Hy Simpson into the shade of the spring house. Fogarty went among the saddlebags, which were those capacious army-issue kind with a large flap and three buckled straps.

McGregor went out back to the trough to strip off his shirt and sluice water over his head. By the time he had finished and was sitting out there to dry off, Hugh came along also to scrub off dirt and sweat. They looked at each other solemnly, and McGregor laughed. "You look like something a pup would drag out of a tanyard. You even smell like it."

Hugh said nothing as he stripped to the waist and ducked to fling on water. He was making noises like a shoat caught under a gate when James asked how his leg was. Hugh tossed water off before replying. "Sore, but not as sore as it was walkin' out yonder, then having to run back to save your oatmeal carcass."

McGregor was startled. "*Oatmeal* carcass?"

Hugh sat down to dry by hot sunlight. "That's what you folks ate, wasn't it? I knew a Scotch hide hunter one time. We was pretty good friends. He told me when he was growin' up over there his family'd stuff a sheep's guts with oatmeal and—"

"Sheep's *guts*?" exclaimed McGregor, standing up to put his shirt on. "Sheep's *stomach*!"

"What's the difference?"

McGregor put an antagonistic look upon his old friend, said nothing until his shirt was buttoned, then went stamping in the direction of the barn as he said, "The difference is that you're so ignorant you wouldn't never understand if I explained it to you. It's sheep's *stomach*, and it's called *haggis*!"

Hugh watched his friend depart, got a cud into his cheek, and ran a hand upward to explore the lump on the side of his face. It was still there, a discolored swelling, but it was no longer feverish to the touch. He flexed his sore knee. It was not as sore as it had been. He spat, eyed the loose horses out a wary distance eating grass, sighed, and arose just as someone rang a triangle over at the main house.

His knee did not hurt at all as he bypassed the barn on his way to the first decent meal he'd had since the Lord knew when.

The interior of the house was a mess. Billy's father said the outlaws had gone through everything looking for money. But they hadn't prized up the kitchen floorboards where the Howes had their cache.

The last man to enter the kitchen was Marshal Fogarty. He had a weathered saddlebag over one shoulder, which he wordlessly dumped in a corner as he sat down to the meal the Mexican and the elder Howe had put together. Hugh pointed with the knife he was using to carry meat and potatoes to his mouth. "Is the loot in there?"

Fogarty was picking up eating utensils when he replied. "Yeah. How much did Whitten say they got?"

"Thirty-five thousand dollars, as I recall. Why?"

"Because there's twenty-five in those bags, not thirty-five."

Nothing was added to this until everyone had begun to flesh out like a toad. Roger Ames set a jug of white lightning on the table as the Mexican began clearing away dishes. Ames said, "Maybe they buried part of it. Or hid it in the rocks out yonder somewhere."

Fogarty nodded and began filling two plates with food for the prisoners they had left chained in the barn. Hugh took cups and a pan of coffee as he followed the lawman.

Jack Porter, the man who had killed the Sheridan livery barn hostler, was slumped, filthy and demoralized, but Whitten was worse off. He had an outsized headache, his eyes were bloodshot, and he was holding a canteen in his lap from which he took frequent long pulls.

Whitten shook his head as Fogarty offered him food. He looked up and asked if there was any whiskey. Joe struck out for the house to fetch back a cupful from the jug.

Hugh Pepperdine leaned on the saddle pole watching Jack Porter eat. He had a vivid flashback to the Sheridan roadway when Porter had turned casually, walked back, and hit the hostler across the top of the head with his six-gun, then just as coolly returned to his horse and rode southward out of town.

Porter looked up. He had pale tan eyes and dark hair. Now he also had dark stubble covering most of his face. He saw Hugh steadily eyeing him and went back to eating. Hugh addressed the other survivor. "Whitten, how much loot did you say you fellers got?"

"Something like thirty-five thousand dollars."

The Canadian's head came up quickly. He glared. "What the hell are you talking about? Who told you that? Not Hy an' not me. We counted it right after supper last night."

Whitten's misery did not prevent him from firing back a waspish retort. "All right then. Just how damned much was there?"

"*Twenty*-five thousand."

Whitten was sullenly unimpressed. "What difference does it make? I kept tellin' you 'n' Hy we'd ought to head one way or another but not straight south. Didn't I?"

Jack Porter drained his coffee cup as Fogarty returned with the whiskey for Carl Whitten. Porter held out his cup. "He don't need all that, mister."

Hugh leaned, struck the cup out of the extended hand, and smiled wolfishly at the surprised Canadian. After Fogarty passed the cup of liquor to Carl Whitten, Hugh looked down at Porter, his smile gone, his eyes like stones.

"You don't know me. I'm the harness an' saddle maker up at Sheridan. I was watchin' you across the road when you 'n' the liveryman's helper was sitting on the bench talking. I saw you hit him as hard as you could over the top of the head with your gun barrel. You killed him."

Porter's eyes sprang to the leaning, relaxed form of big Marshal Fogarty. He found no pity there, so he began scraping at what scraps of food remained on his plate and would not look up at all.

Carl Whitten finished the whiskey, made a horrible grimace, and offered Hugh the empty cup. Pepperdine took it and poked Whitten in the chest with a stiff finger. "Even rattlesnakes'd say thanks if they knew how."

Whitten's eyes were brightening. "Thank you, mister. I appreciate that. I'm beginnin' to feel better already. By the way, who hit me over the head?"

"I did."

"I ain't surprised. First your partner, then you."

Hugh straightened up. "But you're still alive, you miserable bastard, an' in my view you don't deserve to be. That livery barn hostler never did anyone any harm, and he's dead. For a plugged centavo I'd hang the pair of you an' pay for the privilege."

Joe Fogarty scowled at Pepperdine and jerked his head. They started back across the yard, unmindful that the sun was sinking and that a little vagrant late-day breeze was reducing the temperature noticeably. Hugh said, "Where the hell are those livery horses we hired back in Bordenton?"

"Somewhere around. In the morning Billy and his uncle can find them for us."

Hugh looked relieved. "I was scairt you'd want to head back tonight."

Fogarty turned his head. "With you two banged and bumped and sore?"

"McGregor . . . ?"

"Ask him."

"What happened?"

"The first time he pulled both triggers at the same time the old gun knocked him against the saddle pole like he'd been kicked by a mule. The second time he got all braced and the recoil just tipped him over backward. He landed on the back of his head."

"He never said a word about them things to me, Joe."

Fogarty smiled without a lot of mirth. "Hugh, I know how long you and James have been friends. I also know you'd lie to him about being hurt and he'd lie to you the same way. Maybe don't neither of you want the other to think he's not the toughest. I don't know."

They halted on the porch where the dead outlaw had been. Like the others, he was now down in the cool spring house. Fogarty started to go inside and nearly collided with James McGregor, who was coming out. James was nursing a thick crockery mug of whiskey. He went to a bench and eased down very gingerly, saluted Hugh, and drank the whiskey. When he lowered the cup he said, "I'd give a ten-dollar gold piece not to have to ride that livery horse back to Bordenton before we can catch a stage home."

Hugh leaned on the railing. "Back hurt, huh?" he asked solicitously.

McGregor shoved the cup toward Pepperdine as though it were a handgun. "Have a drink," he snarled. "No, my back don't hurt!"

Hugh took two swallows and handed the cup back. "You're hard as nails, James. Tougher'n a boiled owl . . . Along with bein' a cranky old goat, an' right now you're not tellin' the truth."

McGregor peered into the cup, half drained it, and held it out again. "Oatmeal carcass," he snorted. "Finish that up an' go get us another cupful."

Hugh entered the house and McGregor tried several different positions on the bench without finding a comfortable one. When Hugh returned he was sitting very erect with his hips and shoulders against the house wall. It did not look natural, but Hugh ignored it to mention something else.

"The marshal's been going over stuff from them saddlebags. Every one of those screwts was carryin' a wanted poster on himself. Now, what kind of a man would carry something with his picture on it that said he was wanted for a crime an' there was bounty money out on him?"

James was holding their mutual whiskey cup. "An idiotic one, I'd guess; fellers who like to see their picture on things." He sipped whiskey and looked up. "Bounty money?"

"Joe figured it up. Amounts to close to six thousand dollars. They're wanted from Montana all the way to our country. They've robbed banks and trains, killed folks, raided mail stages." Hugh accepted the cup and raised it. "I got to ask Whitten how they got mattresses to put in front of the safes they blew open. Come on down there with me."

"Naw. In the morning. I can tell you how they did

that. They stole mattresses from the rooming house, lugged 'em down the back alley, and stacked 'em in front of the—"

"From the rooming house? How do you know that?"

"I was in the barn with 'em. Remember? After the lad and I killed that raunchy one and the Canadian give up, I stuck a barrel under his chin and asked him. He said that's how they always done it. He also said it was easier at Sheridan than most places because some towns didn't fall for the camp·meetin' trick. They sure as hell did in Sheridan."

McGregor held out his hand. "Don't hog it, Hugh."

Pepperdine handed the cup over. Billy's uncle ambled out where it was cool and stopped to build and light a smoke before joining Hugh in leaning on the railing. He casually said, "If you gents would care to lie over for a couple of weeks an' lend a hand rounding up strays, Billy's paw says he'd pay you tophand wages."

Hugh and James stared at Roger Ames. Without a word they took their cup of popskull down to the barn, growled at the chained prisoners in the gathering gloom, and climbed the loft ladder up where it was darker than the inside of a well.

Up there they shared the whiskey until it was gone, burrowed into fragrant meadow hay, and if the Second Coming had occurred during the night, golden light, clarion trumpets, and all, they would have missed the entire thing.

CHAPTER SEVENTEEN

Questions About Money

Grandpaw Howe and the Mexican were first-rate ranch cooks. There was enough food on the kitchen table to feed half a company of soldiers, and afterward they made up individual bundles and passed them around. Hugh Pepperdine hefted his bundle and smiled. He was properly appreciative. McGregor was, too, for once without limiting his expressions of gratitude.

While Hugh and James were caring for the Bordenton livery animals that Billy had brought in earlier, Marshal Fogarty filled one set of saddlebags with the personal effects of the defunct outlaws and struck up a trade with Billy's father: In exchange for burying the outlaws he could keep the horses and saddles the outlaws had been riding. When Billy's father hesitated, Marshal Fogarty threw in the weapons and Billy's father shook on it.

They got away from the yard with their prisoners shortly before daybreak and were out more than a mile when Fogarty looked back to fix in his mind that ranch where he'd survived something that equaled just about any other scrape he could remember living through in his lifetime.

He had a rangeman's facility for recovering from hardship. Sleep and plenty of food had contributed, but it went deeper than that. From childhood to this, his thirty-fifth year, Joe Fogarty had lived hard.

He did not, however, look very presentable. None of them did. They had scraggly beards, their faces were burned bronze, their lips were cracked, they were tucked up from weariness and dehydration, their clothing was filthy, and their faces showed clear vestiges of what they had been through. Even after that big breakfast, Fogarty'd had to take up his britches belt two notches.

The prisoners looked the worst. They were completely demoralized. Neither of them opened their mouths during the ride back through those scab-rock hills. When the full day's heat arrived, Whitten looked downright ill, so they favored him at waterholes and shady places. He would drink water but still refused food.

Even McGregor, who despised outlaws, lost a little of his natural flintiness. He rode with Whitten and from time to time soaked a filthy neckerchief which he had tied around the injured man's head. Whitten did not appear to appreciate this even though as time passed he was able to sit straighter in his saddle, at least temporarily.

For many miles there was little more than grunts from any of them. By the time they broke out of those inhospitable rocky low hills and got down parallel to the stage road where the heat beat directly upon them, Whitten seemed to lapse into periods of disorientation.

Hugh rode on one side of him, McGregor on the other side. Marshal Fogarty rode behind his prisoners. Even though they appeared harmless, experience had taught Joe never to slacken vigilance when bringing in outlaws.

The sun was slanting away when they had Bordenton in sight as a shimmery, miragelike scattering of buildings that appeared to alternately be closer, then farther.

They made their last rest halt at a stagecoach turnout where there was a log trough and tree shade. Here they hobbled the animals, sank down in shade, and ate from the bundles the Howe ranch had provided. Afterward, when Carl Whitten rolled onto his side and slept, the others did the same. They would be in Bordenton before nightfall even if they rested for a couple of hours.

There was no traffic. In midsummer everyone including travelers did as much as they could before the sun climbed, and as little as possible until the sun was gone in early evening.

McGregor was washing at the trough when Pepperdine awakened, stifled a groan as he sat up, and got stiffly upright to head for the trough. McGregor looked up, then continued dousing his clothing with water. As Hugh leaned to cool his face, the gunsmith said, "How hard did you hit Whitten?"

Hugh flung off water to gaze over where the injured outlaw was sleeping. "No harder than he hit me. Why, you think I busted his skull?"

McGregor ran bent fingers through his wet gingery hair before replying. "Maybe. I don't know. He sure don't act right though."

Joe Fogarty herded the Canadian to the trough to sluice off as the harness maker said, "Maybe he's got one of them eggshell skulls."

The Canadian looked up with water running off his face, twisted to look back where the injured outlaw was still sleeping, and snorted but went back to washing and soaking his clothing without speaking.

Fogarty went over to rouse Whitten. The outlaw rolled onto his back looking up at the big man above him and made a bubbly groan. Joe helped him to his feet. Whitten clung to the lawman's arm without attempting to walk for several seconds. Fogarty had some whiskey in one of the saddlebags and left Whitten to get it.

The outlaw sank to the ground with his head in his hands. Joe got some whiskey down Whitten, but as they rigged out to ride the last few miles to Bordenton, Whitten sat slumped and motionless.

They had to help him astride. McGregor encouraged the outlaw with kind words and rode beside him when they left the turnout heading due northward on the roadbed. The sun was gone, but at this time of year daylight lingered until about nine o'clock. What made the final leg of their trip bearable was that without direct sunlight the heat was noticeably less.

It was dusk when they turned in at the Bordenton livery barn. The possum-bellied proprietor was not on hand, but his nighthawk was. He was a rawboned, gray man as ugly as original sin with tobacco stains on the droopy dragoon mustache that hid most of his mouth.

He showed no surprise at all as he wordlessly led the horses down the runway where Fogarty removed the saddlebags, took McGregor's long-barreled rifle, and herded his prisoners up the roadway in the direction of the jailhouse. Carl Whitten clung to Jack Porter as they walked up ahead and halted in front of the dark jailhouse.

Joe entered first, lighted the coal-oil lamp, hung it from its ceiling wire, and dumped the bags in a corner behind the scuffed table that had served Bordenton's lawman as a desk for many years.

They helped Whitten to a bunk, locked both prisoners

in, and went over to the cafe, which was empty because suppertime had come and gone more than an hour earlier. The same cafeman who had fed them before did it again, his eyes lively with interest, but he wisely asked no questions.

They were concentrating on their meal when two men came in from out front, sat down, and gazed at the three disreputable diners from Sheridan, who did not even look up from eating.

One of the newcomers said, "Glad you gents got back."

Fogarty looked up to his right, swallowed, and nodded. "We are too, Mayor. We expected to see some riders from Bordenton down yonder. In fact, we was sort of counting on it."

The blacksmith pursed his lips and said nothing until the cafeman had set a crockery mug of black java in front of him. "Well, some fellers did ride out yestiddy. When they came back in the evening they said it was no use, that all the tracks they found was on the roadway, and there was too many to tell one from the others."

Bert Stiles sipped coffee. Evidently, it was too hot, or possibly too bitter, because he pushed the cup aside and leaned on the counter. "Did you find 'em?" he asked Marshal Fogarty, and got a nod unaccompanied by words because Joe was eating again.

The blacksmith studied the three men for a while in silence. "You found 'em. Well now, that's real good news. An' you found our money, too, did you?"

McGregor paused between mouthfuls to put a cold gaze upon the blacksmith. Then he ignored the man and resumed eating.

Stiles reddened slightly, which none of the eating men noticed because they were concentrating on their supper.

The other man who had entered with Stiles was on the opposite end of the counter bench a short distance from Hugh. He had been listening up to this point, but now he spoke.

His voice was husky and wavery. "There's a reward, gents. Two hundred dollars for the return of our money."

Hugh looked around. It was the local banker, and he was sweating even though it had not been hot enough for that in a couple of hours. The banker's carefully trimmed beard, coarse features, and hooded, hawklike eyes put Hugh in mind of a cornered falcon. "How much did they get, Mr. Sanford?"

The hooded eyes slid away then back. "Enough. Enough to maybe ruin the town."

Joe Fogarty put down his knife and fork and leaned to look around the harness maker. "My partner here asked you a direct question. *How much did your bank lose?*"

The blacksmith interrupted to say, "Nine thousand dollars in round figures. Did you boys recover any money off those bastards?"

Hugh was after the banker again and ignored Bert Stiles. "Mr. Sanford, are you plumb sure you can throw money around like that? A two-hunnert-dollar reward to get back nine thousand dollars. You got to be one of them folks that's all heart."

Hugh stabbed at his meat and went back to eating, mad as a hornet.

The blacksmith tried his coffee again, and again rejected it. He fished out a huge tan handkerchief and mopped sweat off his face, growled when the cafeman offered to refill his coffee cup, and as the cafeman departed, the blacksmith said, "Three hundred, gents. If you got our money back."

Without looking up from his plate or swallowing a

mouthful of supper, James McGregor said, "Five hundred. Fetch it over to the jailhouse. Take your time, gents. You got half an hour."

They arose, tossed down silver, and walked out of the cafe with the cafeman, the mayor, and the banker staring after them. The cafeman said, "Are you going to let them get away with holdin' up the town like that?"

Stiles arose, darkly angry. "Shut up," he exclaimed, and drove the banker outside in front of him. Out there he said, "Well . . . ?"

Amos Sanford put his back to the lighted jailhouse and snarled at the blacksmith. "Five hundred dollars. What do you think I'm goin' to do?"

"How do we know they got our money?"

Sanford's snarl sharpened. "We don't *know*. I think they got it. You come up to the bank with me while I get five hundred dollars, then we go back to the jailhouse, an' if they got it, they get the five hundred."

"An' if they don't have it?"

"Oh, for chrissake, Bert. *They got it. I know they got it.* Now come along."

In the middle of the week Bordenton had slightly more activity than Sheridan had, but only because it was a larger town with more outlets for nighttime release. Even so, as James McGregor went out front to sit in darkness on the wooden bench bolted to the jailhouse front wall, the town seemed particularly quiet to him.

He was still out there when he heard marching footsteps approaching from the north. He arose, went inside, told Marshal Fogarty he thought they were coming, and Hugh Pepperdine grinned from ear to ear.

McGregor was correct. The town's mayor and its banker walked in out of darkness, blinked a little, and squinted when bright lamplight hit their eyes and Marshal Fogarty arose from behind the old table, expressionless and silent. In front of him was nine thousand dollars in stacks of neatly squared greenbacks.

Amos Sanford felt for a chair without taking his eyes off the money. Bert Stiles's interest went further. He was viewing the squared stacks when he said, "Altogether, how much money did you recover, Marshal?"

Fogarty fixed the blacksmith with a cool stare. "All you gents got to worry about is getting your nine thousand back. Mr. Sanford, where is the five hundred?"

The banker arose, groped inside his coat, pulled out a packet of greenbacks, and placed it on the table. "It's all there, but you're welcome to count it."

Fogarty briefly glanced at the money the banker had put down, then returned his attention to the blacksmith. "Seems to you like a lot of money for a little riding, don't it?"

Stiles glanced at the two older men, battered, rumpled, and none-too-clean-looking. He slowly shook his head. "I guess not. Anyone get hurt?"

"We got two prisoners in your cell room. We're taking them up to Sheridan in the morning. Yes, there were some men got hurt. Five got killed."

The banker's eyes jumped to Marshal Fogarty's face and stayed there until he pushed up out of the chair, approached the desk, and began stuffing his nine thousand dollars into his coat pockets as he spoke to Bordenton's mayor. "Bert, give me a hand here."

The blacksmith approached the desk and went to work stuffing pockets. He showed no emotion until they were finished. As the banker went to the roadway door, Mayor Stiles looked at the men from Sheridan and nodded in what could have been approval. "That's a hunnert dollars a killing. That's about the goin' rate, I expect." He paused in the doorway. "Bordenton's obliged, gents."

He closed the door after himself. Hugh and James McGregor, who had been standing throughout all this, went to a wall bench and sank down. Joe Fogarty sat down in the chair behind the table and smiled.

"They're going to sweat," he said. "Nine thousand dollars and a busted safe to keep it in." Neither of the older men spoke. Fogarty arose. "I'll get some grub for the prisoners, then I expect one of us had better find out when the first stage leaves town in the morning. We better sleep right here in the jailhouse."

Fogarty left the office, aiming toward the cafe. Hugh dug for a coin and flipped it as he said, "Call it."

McGregor obeyed. "Heads."

He won. Hugh sighed, pocketed the coin, and walked out into the pleasant night, heading for the stage company's corralyard.

McGregor went after a drink of water from a hanging olla. He returned to the bench, eased his back against the wall, and blew out a rattling big sigh.

When Fogarty returned with two pails, one of stew, the other of black coffee, he and McGregor took the food down into the cell room.

Jack Porter met them at the door, where they handed in the pails. McGregor was still solicitous about Carl Whitten and asked the Canadian how he was. Porter said, "Better. He's still drinkin' a lot of water, but an hour or so back he sat up and made a smoke. Right now he's sleepin' again. I'd say he's in pretty good shape after havin' someone try to kill him by hittin' him real hard over the skull."

When the lawman and gunsmith returned to the office

and Hugh returned from the stage office, they did not tell him what the Canadian had said. It didn't matter anyway as long as Whitten was on the mend.

The first northbound stage out of Bordenton would leave at five o'clock in the morning. Hugh completed this announcement with another one. "You want to guess who the driver is? Jack Carpenter, same feller who brought us down here."

Fogarty and McGregor were indifferent to this bit of trivia. The three of them divided that five hundred dollars, then locked the jailhouse from the inside, took a lamp down into the cell room, and bedded down. When Jack Porter would have struck up a conversation, Marshal Fogarty told him to shut his damned mouth.

CHAPTER EIGHTEEN

Heading North

Daylight was close when they got their prisoners into the coach, wasted ten minutes renewing the acquaintance of the driver, whose inebriation had been the cause of their day-long "rest" in the Bordenton *juzgado*, got all the guns and saddlebags crammed inside, closed the door, and whistled to Carpenter that they were ready.

They hadn't eaten nor had the customary morning coffee, so they were not very talkative as the driver talked up his hitch, cut a big sashay clear of the gates, and walked his horses with slack traces to the upper end of town and for a short way beyond before easing them up against their collar pads.

Carl Whitten's eyes were brighter today, but he still looked like he'd been yanked through a knothole. His color was gray, his injuries were still discolored and swollen, his sunken, unshaven cheeks were covered with beard stubble that was partly gray, partly red, and partly brown.

Whitten's clear signs of recovery made McGregor revert to his earlier dourness. When Whitten smiled at

157

him and said he appreciated James's help on the ride up to Bordenton, McGregor replied exactly as he would have if he'd never pitied the renegade. "Seemed a shame to me that you might die before you got hanged."

After that Carl Whitten avoided saying anything to the Sheridan gunsmith.

They made their first rest stop with the sun climbing and the promise of heat later manifesting itself as it usually did; the air was without any of the freshness it had had earlier when there'd been dewy moisture in it.

Jack Carpenter was silently forgiven for the discomfort he'd caused back in Bordenton, for he produced a small, stout wicker hamper from the boot, and while his horses hung in their harness after being watered, content to doze as long as they could, Carpenter handed out cold fried chicken and tomatoes from his wife's garden. He filled five tin cups with coffee still hot from being insulated in the gallon jug by having three layers of croaker sacking sewed around it.

He beamed at their gratitude. "Well, they told me last night who I'd be taking north this morning, and since my brother-in-law the cafeman don't even fire up his stove until six o'clock, I figured you gents'd be hungry." He was refilling the Canadian's cup when he also said, "To tell you the truth, Bordenton didn't treat you fellers very well. This here was my wife's idea as much as mine."

Pepperdine spoke around a mouthful of cold fried chicken. "You're a lucky man, Mr. Carpenter. Don't very many men get wives like yours."

The whip nodded his head. "That's the truth; she'll be pleased to hear what you said. Have some coffee."

Joe Fogarty ate mostly in silence, eyeing his prisoners. When the Canadian met his gaze, Joe asked a question. "How long was Hy Simpson at the outlaw's trade?"

Porter chewed, washed meat down with black coffee, then replied. "I'm not sure. Carl could answer better'n I could. I just joined up a few months before we started raidin' toward the Mex line."

Whitten said, "Hy come from back east somewhere. I heard him say one time he got started in Illinois when he was kind of young. Then he went out to Nebraska and by the time he got this far west he'd worked out some real good ideas for robbing banks and all."

"How long were you with him?" Fogarty asked.

Whitten rinsed his mouth with java and spat aside. "Three years."

"Ever get chased?"

"Hell, yes, just about every time we'd stop a stage or rob a bank. But Hy figured things ahead. One time in Montana, half the damned countryside was beatin' the brush for us after a mine robbery. Hy led us to a grove where he'd hid an emigrant wagon. We turned the horses loose and piled everything inside under the bedding. That feller who was the preacher up at Sheridan, he dressed up like a woman, with a bonnet and all, and you know, them possemen stopped us once and let us go. Otherwise we saw 'em chargin' all over the countryside like hornets when a man hits their nest with a stick." Whitten brightened at the recollection. "We drove that old wagon right through 'em and out of the country. Marshal, Hy was a real master. This time he was makin' us rich as we went toward Messico. He'd already made plans down there to buy a big ranch where we'd be safe an' comfortable for a couple of years."

McGregor washed in the trough, dried his hands on the outside of his trouser legs, and helped the driver store things back in the hamper. He would not even look at Carl Whitten or Jack Porter.

When they left the shady turnout and were back on the road heading north again, Hugh eyed his old friend with tolerant amusement. McGregor, for his part, rode looking out at the countryside. The last time they'd made this trip, in reverse, it had been too dark to see much.

The longest haul was from this point on. Inside, despite a thick, reinforced roof which, it was claimed, kept out the heat, the old coach felt like an oven. They had two water jugs, courtesy of the stage line. By midafternoon Hugh shook his head, saying it was like drinking a man's own bathwater. But it was wet.

With the sun sliding off-center, the whip favored his horses until he had the last turnout in sight, then he let them trot.

This time when they stopped there was nothing to eat, but the trough water was cold, so they dampened their shirts, poured water over their heads from their hats, and spent fifteen minutes resting.

Carl Whitten sprawled beneath a black oak and snored. His companion, the Canadian, who had been increasingly silent as they got closer to Sheridan, eyed Marshal Fogarty from time to time. Whether Joe noticed this or not, Hugh did.

As they were climbing back into the coach, Hugh managed to be directly behind the Canadian. When Porter stepped up and ducked low, Hugh tapped him on the back. "You got a thick skull?" he asked quietly.

When the rig was moving again, Jack Porter studied Hugh Pepperdine more than he studied the lawman. Hugh seemed to always be looking at him when Porter glanced in his direction.

The driver leaned once to call downward. "Bunch of riders to the west. You see them?"

Everyone leaned to look out on that side as Carpenter whistled his horses up into a steady trot.

It was difficult to count the distant riders because they were riding all in a bunch, but their course was roughly parallel to the stagecoach, on a northeasterly angle which, if they held to it, was going to put them slightly ahead of the stagecoach within about a mile.

Sheridan was not yet in sight, but it was no more than three or four miles ahead.

Joe Fogarty was watching the converging horsemen when he said, "Rangemen heading for town, maybe. What day is it?"

No one knew, but if it was Saturday, then those men out yonder most likely were indeed stockmen heading for Sheridan and Rusty Morton's saloon. If it wasn't Saturday, and those men didn't veer off, they were going to intercept the stage about two miles south of town.

Wordlessly, James McGregor picked up his shotgun, checked the loads, and rode with the gun across his lap as he watched the riders.

Hugh Pepperdine leaned toward the gunsmith. "What would you say the range was?"

McGregor turned quickly. "Less'n a mile, Hugh."

Pepperdine took one of the long-barreled rifles and, with Fogarty as well as the two prisoners watching, hauled back the dog, lifted the trapdoor, saw the big brass casing, closed the trapdoor, and eased down the dog as he leaned across in front of McGregor to rest the barrel on the left-side opening in front of the rattling door.

Marshal Fogarty started to speak, but McGregor cut

him off. "Leave him be, Joe. If they figure to stop this coach, this ought to change their minds."

Hugh's sighting would have been better if the stagecoach hadn't been rocking along at a trot, but since his idea did not call for accuracy, when he squeezed the trigger the bullet threw up a gout of small stones, dirt, and dust about ten yards in front of the loping horsemen. Their reaction was immediate and prudent. They yanked back to a sliding halt, obviously as astonished at the range of the shot as at its unexpectedness.

Inside the coach the explosion was deafening. Outside, it brought a loud squawk from Carpenter up on his high seat, who was suddenly called upon to use all his experience to keep the abruptly alarmed horses from taking their bits in their teeth and running.

Carpenter was cursing at the top of his voice as his outfit swiftly outdistanced the astonished horsemen. He did not even glance in their direction for another mile, by which time Sheridan's rooftops were in sight.

Inside the coach McGregor was smiling broadly as he and the other passengers watched those horsemen resume their course toward the stage road, but this time at a dead walk. The Canadian outlaw said something that had not occupied the thoughts of his companions, but which, after he said it, took root. "Gawddamned lynchers. Sure as hell they was aiming to stop the stage up yonder."

Joe Fogarty watched Hugh shuck the spent brass casing, pitch it out of the coach, and plug in a fresh load. When their eyes met, Hugh smiled a little. "If it's Saturday, nobody got hurt. If it ain't Saturday—well, still nobody got hurt," he said.

The big lawman leaned far out to look back. The driver up above was doing the same thing now that he had his horses under control. He yelled at Fogarty, "Who are they?"

Fogarty did not answer.

Carpenter faced forward, redfaced and sweating, but satisfied that whatever those riders had in mind about riding toward a point of juncture with his outfit on the roadway, whoever down there had blown up rocks and dust in front of them at a range of close to what Carpenter figured had to be a mile, had sure as God made little green apples changed their minds.

Dusk was approaching, slowly and inexorably. The heat had not diminished very much, which probably meant the night was going to be one of those hot ones right up until close to dawn.

Sheridan's lights glowed a soft welcome as Jack Carpenter walked his animals the last mile to have them properly cooled out before he reached the corralyard.

It was about suppertime; there were very few people on the plank walks as the old stagecoach went up through town as far as the scuffed old palisaded corralyard gateposts and turned in.

Two yardmen were getting the lighted lantern hauled up to the top of the cedar log in the center of the yard, which was supposed to aid visibility but which did so only providing a coach halted directly beneath it, and even then shadows distorted everything. Still, until the moon rose, that lantern was better than nothing at all.

Fogarty alighted first and stood aside as his prisoners came down. Hugh and McGregor were slower disembarking. They had James's arsenal to take out. They also tossed out the saddlebags the marshal had brought along. When the coach was finally unloaded, those two yardmen began taking the horses off the pole, working in silence as they did this.

It was too dark for evening strollers, of whom there were very few, to notice that three men carrying guns and saddlebags in the direction of the Sheridan jailhouse were herding along two other men with neither saddlebags nor weapons.

As soon as Hugh and James saw Joe Fogarty drive his prisoners down into the cell room to be locked up, they jettisoned everything they had been carrying but McGregor's weapons and went back out into the hot evening.

Up at the gun shop, where they placed the weapons atop the counter, McGregor lighted a lamp and said, "You want to start collecting that week of drinks I owe you tonight?"

Pepperdine shook his head. "Maybe tomorrow night. Right now I want to pump my washtub full and set in it for an hour, then lather all over and set in it for another hour. Then shave and see if I got any clean clothes. After that I'm goin' to sleep the clock around."

McGregor did an uncharacteristic thing. He slapped his old friend on the shoulder as he said, "See you maybe tomorrow, or maybe the next day. Good night."

When Pepperdine closed the shop door after himself and struck out at an angle for his harness works on the opposite side of the roadway, McGregor blew out his lamp, went to a front window, and watched his old friend heading for home.

He did not see four men emerge from Morton's saloon, on the same side of Main Street as his shop, and stand in darkness watching Hugh's progress.

CHAPTER NINETEEN

Getting Hoorawed

Hugh was leaning to fit the key into his shop door when those four men over in front of the saloon started past the hitchrack, heading in his direction. He had the key inserted and was turning it, when a sharp, hard voice said, "You old son of a bitch!"

Hugh was so startled he did not even begin turning until the four rangemen were close enough to step up onto the plank walk.

The man who had spoken was large and bulky with a mouth like a bear trap, which was about all Hugh could see of him, except for a sweaty old hat, a faded blue shirt, and dark trousers. Behind this man the other three were standing slouched and hostile.

Hugh said, "You talking to me?"

The bulky man's reply was a snarl. "Yeah. If you're the harness maker who was on that stage Jack Carpenter was driving this afternoon, an' who took a rifle shot at us."

Hugh's surprise had passed. He was armed—and so were they, all four of them. The bulky man stepped up

165

onto the duckboards. "What's the matter with you, you darned old fool? If your aim had been better, you'd have hit someone."

"Mister," stated Pepperdine, "if I'd figured to aim better, you're dead right. That shot was to warn you fellers away from meeting the stage on the road."

"Why? You afraid of some fellers hoorawing the stage a little?"

"No. I've been hoorawed before. Today we had two prisoners in the coach, along with Marshal Fogarty, me 'n' a friend of mine. We'd just come back from some shooting trouble. For all we knew, you was lynchers."

One of the cowboys behind the bulky man sneered. "Shooting trouble! An old goat like you?"

The bulky man stepped closer to Hugh, and the harness maker let his right hand hover above his holster. The bulky man showed white teeth in the gloom. "You wouldn't draw that thing, would you, harness maker?" He lashed out so fast that even if it had not been too dark for Hugh to see the blow coming, he could not have avoided being struck.

Pepperdine was slammed against the door at his back so hard the knob gouged him. He was dazed for five seconds. One of the men farther back said, "Bust him in two, Jed, an' let's get back to the saloon."

Hugh's vision cleared as the bulky man set himself for a belly blow. He was starting to twist sideways to avoid the blow when his bad knee gave way and he started to stagger and fall.

The bulky man's rock-hard fist caught Hugh in the side as he was going down. From across the road a gravelly voice sang out, "Step back, you son of a bitch. Get away from him."

The four rangemen turned. Another older man was

nearing the center of the road on his march from the gun shop. He was holding a short-barreled shotgun in his hands, both hammers hauled back.

"You deaf?" McGregor snarled. "I said get away from the door. Move back into the road. *Move!*" McGregor halted in the middle of the starlit road, both barrels of his scattergun aimed directly at the rigid range riders.

One of them started shuffling away from the plank walk. He was being very careful that both arms were held away from his sides. The other two men who had not been on the plank walk did the same, which left the bulky man, who had not moved.

Only a complete fool would not obey orders given from something like a hundred feet away by someone holding a cocked shotgun. At that range McGregor's weapon could cut a man in two.

The bulky man stepped sideways off the plank walk out into the manured dust of the road. All four rangemen were as motionless and still as stones.

McGregor did not take his eyes off them as he said, "Hugh, are you all right?"

Pepperdine was back on his feet, but with most of his weight on the leg that had not been injured earlier. He ignored the question to say, "Those are the men we saw trying to overtake the stage this afternoon, James."

The burly man held both hands away from his sides, palms forward. "What the hell, we was just out to have a little fun. Maybe hooraw you boys on the way to town."

McGregor was not appeased, but for a while he was silent. There were a few spectators southward, well clear of the range of the scattergun. A few more appeared here and there, and one man loped to the lighted jailhouse office.

McGregor said, "Hugh? Hurt your leg again?"

"Yeah. A little."

The gunsmith walked slowly closer to the round-eyed rangemen, halted, and lowered both barrels of his weapon until they were belt-buckle high on the burly man. "What's your name?" he asked.

"Jed Holbert. These here fellers work for me. I own an outfit west of Sheridan about nine miles. Bought it last spring."

McGregor's blue eyes were merciless in the gloom. "Mr. Holbert, I don't give a damn where you came from, but in Sheridan country we don't come up on a man from behind and hit him." McGregor was thoughtfully silent for another short period, then said, "Shuck your guns. All of you. Now then, Mr. Holbert, we like jokes, too, so you just shed that coat and hat. *Shed 'em!*"

The burly man obeyed.

"Fine. Now your britches and shirt."

Jed Holbert stared. McGregor took one more forward step. The twin shotgun barrels were about six feet from the bulky man's stomach. "I'll blow you out of 'em, Mr. Holbert!"

The rangeman slowly unbuttoned his shirt and dropped it. He lowered his hands to his sides and glared at McGregor. Hugh called from the harness-works doorway, "You better do it, cowman. Day before yestiddy I saw Mr. McGregor blow a man apart with that gun."

Holbert began to fumblingly unbuckle his belt, unbutton his britches, and let them fall. He was naked except for a soiled pair of white drawers. He was also scarlet in the face, but that was not visible in the night.

An angry roar from southward in the roadway broke the silence. "James, what the hell do you think you're doing!" Joe Fogarty stamped up to them and stopped, legs wide and furious. "Are you crazy?"

Hugh answered from the doorway. "Those are the fellers who was going to hooraw the stage this afternoon, Joe. That one without his pants, he come up behind me and started workin' me over."

Fogarty twisted from the waist. It was difficult to make out Pepperdine in the doorway. "Are you hurt?" he asked.

"Well, I got a sore back from a doorknob and some sore ribs."

"How's your leg?"

"Twisted it again."

Fogarty faced the bulky man. "Who are you?" After Holbert answered, the marshal glanced at the other range riders, at their weapons lying in the roadway, then back at the bulky man. "You live around here?"

"Bought a cow outfit about nine, ten miles west of here last spring."

"Where are you from?"

"Texas."

Fogarty stood a while gazing at the other large man, then swung. The strike sounded like a distant gunshot. Jed Holbert was falling before Joe's arm was back at his side. His riders neither moved nor made a sound. Fogarty gestured to them. "Pick him up and carry him down to the jailhouse. *I said pick him up!*"

As the cowboys were obeying, Marshal Fogarty walked over where Hugh was leaning, studied him, shook his head, and walked back to the center of the road and faced the gunsmith. "James, go home. Put that damned shotgun away and go to bed, will you?"

Instead of obeying, McGregor eased down the hammers of his weapon and went over to the harness-shop doorway. He helped Hugh inside, groped around for the lamp, lighted it, and returned to the doorway to watch the procession walking toward the jailhouse as he said, "Hugh, we're too long in the tooth for this kind of monkey business." He turned, eyed his old friend who was sitting on his sewing horse, and also said, "You got any whiskey around here?"

Two townsmen appeared in the doorway, grinning widely. One of them called to the gunsmith, "I'd have paid ten dollars to see that."

McGregor's reply was tart. "You got to see it free. Now leave us be."

The townsmen went diagonally across the road toward Rusty Morton's saloon. Over there, drinks went around, and laughter reached all the way to the south end of town.

The two older men had just got comfortable in the harness shop with a bottle between them and a pair of sticky glasses in hand when someone out in the darkness began hammering on the door. The noise was both startling and irritating. McGregor shot up to his feet, but Hugh was already limping toward the door as he said, "Set down and relax."

Hugh opened the door and was nearly bowled over by the stocky man who rushed in. "I just heard the commotion. Over at the saloon they're saying you three got back about suppertime." As the stocky man paused for breath, McGregor growled at him from deeper in the shop. "Your damned money is safe, Mr. Donner. It isn't in here. Go down to the jailhouse."

The banker peered past until he found the gunsmith, then he heaved a big sigh. "You got it! By gawd, I told folks around town if anyone could catch those—"

McGregor was on his feet as he interrupted. "I told you. Go see Joe Fogarty. Unless he's locked up for the night, he can tell you the whole story."

The banker's exuberance wilted under the gunsmith's sharpness. As he was turning to leave, he said, "Like I told you, there's a hundred-dollar reward. You boys can pick it up at the bank anytime."

Hugh closed the door, limped back to the sewing horse, got settled, and picked up his glass as he said, "Hundred dollars? I thought it was two hundred."

McGregor leaned for Pepperdine to pour whiskey into his glass. "It was two hundred." He settled back with the refilled glass. "They're all the same, Hugh. Like that droopy-eyed son of a bitch down in Bordenton. It's maybe bred into the bone, otherwise they wouldn't be bankers. How's your leg now?"

It was not so much the leg. It was a little painful, but only when Hugh moved. What was more painful was his back where that doorknob had gouged him over the kidneys. But he shrugged his injuries off, considered his glass, then laughed. "That was about the funniest thing I ever saw. A big cowman with his cowboys to back him up, takin' off his britches in the middle of the roadway. I wish it had been broad daylight." Hugh laughed so long that McGregor got a twinkle in his eye. He downed his jolt and stood up to place the glass on the counter. "You don't suppose we could get some rest now, do you?" He turned to squint toward the roadway through the night-darkened front window. "What the hell else can be out there lyin' in wait?"

Hugh was still tickled, so he said, "Whoever posed for that painting of the fat lady over Rusty's bar."

McGregor went to the door, looked back, wagged his head, and struck out for the gun shop.

Several men idling in the hot night in front of Morton's saloon recognized him, saw the shotgun he was carrying, and spoke quickly but softly back and forth. If McGregor heard them, he gave no indication of it.

He went inside, did not go near the lamp, barred the door, went through to his lean-to off the rear of the shop, and got ready for bed.

The whiskey as much as the recent excitement kept him awake for a long time. Just as he was about to drift off, a sudden thought sprang both his eyes wide open.

Marshal Fogarty had given those horses and outfits to the Howes for burying the bank robbers, and sure as hell three of those horses belonged to those two plaid-shirted angry freighters who had nearly caused a fight in the saloon down in Bordenton.

McGregor flopped onto his back, stared straight upward, and groaned.

CHAPTER TWENTY

Almost Back to Normal

Neither the harness works nor the gun shop opened for business until almost ten o'clock the following morning, an unheard-of state of affairs, and even after the front doors were unlocked, there was no sign of life inside.

Joe Fogarty, scrubbed, shaved, wearing clean clothes, and smelling of the French toilet water the local barber doused customers with, came up to the harness shop a little shy of noon and leaned on the counter to watch Hugh sewing a pigeon-wing saddle skirt. Hugh let the needles hang as he leaned on the high viselike wooden clamps of his sewing horse. "Now what's wrong?" he asked, and before Fogarty could reply, Hugh wagged a finger at him. "Whatever it is, me an' James ain't interested, don't want no part of it, and that's final."

Fogarty leaned, listened, and shrugged. He counted out one hundred dollars atop the counter and put another hundred back into a shirt pocket. "That's your share. The other hundred goes to James. It's Pete Donner's contribution to getting his six thousand dollars back."

Hugh gazed at the money. "Last night he came bustin'

in here and said the total reward was one hundred dollars."

"Well, he was wrong. It was three hundred dollars. One hundred each for you an' me and one hundred for James." Joe straightened up off the counter. "That Texas twister who jumped you last night—he sure must have fallen hard. His jaw is cracked. He looks like someone with the biggest case of mumps you ever saw."

"Did you turn him out?"

"Yeah. With orders not even to drive to Sheridan for groceries for six months, an' if he does an' I catch him, he's goin' to have another lump on the other side of his face."

As Marshal Fogarty was turning toward the door, two large, bearded men wearing plaid shirts walked in. The man in front nodded. "I'm Russ Hamstead. This here is Colin Beasley. You remember us, Marshal? A few nights back down in Bordenton we were tellin' you about thieves makin' off with three of our saddle animals?"

Fogarty and Pepperdine stared at the freighters, then slowly looked at each other.

The freighters came over to the counter to lean. The one named Russ Hamstead squinted his eyes in a smile at Fogarty. "We heard you got back to town last night. They said at the cafe this morning you run them buzzards down and overhauled them a little. We was wonderin' if maybe you got our horses back."

Fogarty stood like a wooden Indian. Hugh raised his voice in a loud welcome and pointed to the iron stove where the speckled coffeepot was simmering. "Made fresh this morning, gents. Help yourselves. Good to see you boys again. I figured you'd be long gone by the time we got back."

Colin Beasley went after a cup of java. "We was

going to, then we heard about you fellers goin' after those bank robbers." He smiled at Hugh. "Sure is fresh coffee. Got a fine flavor to it, friend. . . . Marshal, we'd like to pick up the horses if you brought 'em back and hitch up first thing in the morning to head north. There's talk of a big job up there haulin' rocks for a mine."

Joe Fogarty leaned back against the counter. Surprise did not last too long at any time, not even when it had been as complete as this surprise had been. He smiled at Colin Beasley. "Tell me, just how much was those three horses worth?"

The other freighter replied. "We give thirty dollars a head for them, but they was worth fifty. Easy riding animals, not hard to catch, tough on the road. Does someone want to buy them, Marshal?"

Fogarty studiously avoided Hugh's gaze as he dug in a trouser pocket and withdrew a roll of greenbacks. "I'll give fifty a head for them, Mr. Hamstead."

Not a word was said as Joe counted one hundred and fifty dollars and handed it to the bearded man. Hamstead looked pleased as he reverently folded the money and tucked it away. "You need a bill of sale, Marshal?"

Joe shoved out his big hand. "A handshake will do."

Hamstead shook Fogarty's hand; so did his partner. They were walking toward the door when Hamstead looked back with a smile. "Sure glad we didn't get into a fight the other night, Marshal. This here is a real nice town."

Hugh straddled the sewing horse with his head bowed over folded arms, ribs shaking. Joe Fogarty shoved back his hat, eyed the older man a moment, then said, "There went my hundred from Donner and fifty of my own money."

Hugh raised his head. "It's God's gift, is what it is."

"What are you talking about?"

"The Irish got it. They're born with it. Anyone else would have stammered and stuttered and run with cold sweat. You stood there looking as believable as a preacher weaseling your way out of telling them what you did with their horses."

Fogarty went over to the gun shop, where James McGregor was cleaning his long-barreled rifles and his scattergun. He eyed the lawman askance. "I thought of something bad last night, Marshal. Remember those three horses some freighters said was stole from their camp?"

Fogarty nodded. "I just paid them a hundred and fifty dollars for their damned horses." He fished in a shirt pocket and placed a hundred dollars on the counter. "With Donner's compliments. He upped the ante to three hundred when I gave him back his bank money." Before McGregor started asking questions Marshal Fogarty changed the subject. "I sent off some letters this morning. One to the banks up north that was raided, and some other letters to law agencies putting in for the rewards on Simpson and his friends. I also sent one to the state capital asking them to send a circuit-riding judge down here so we can put Porter and Whitten on trial for murder and robbery. James, I still got about ten thousand dollars in the jailhouse safe."

McGregor was pragmatic. "Someone'll be along. When the word gets around, you'll have to beat off bankers with a stick." James studied his stained hands a moment before speaking again. "Did someone say the bounty money'll add up to about six thousand dollars?"

Joe thought that was roughly the figure. "Give or take

one way or the other. Some of those wanted dodgers are pretty old. Why?"

"Well, you know the bank owns this building. Donner once told me he'd sell it for six hundred dollars."

Fogarty twisted slightly to watch a top buggy go spanking southward in midmorning sunlight. It had yellow running gear and red wheels. He spoke as he watched the rig pass from sight. "It might take a while to get the bounty money, James. In my experience, those things can drag along for up to a year." He faced back around. McGregor was picking at a callus on his right hand. He was faintly smiling.

"I'll wait," he told the lawman. "I'm used to it. Been waiting for something all my life."

Fogarty returned to the roadway, where heat was beginning to build up. There was the usual pedestrian traffic, mostly passing in and out of the general store, where Hank Dennis and his clerk, a wizened, taciturn man who wore black cotton sleeve-protectors that reached from his wrists to his elbows, managed a thriving business. In fact, about half the money robbed from the Sheridan Bank & Trust Company had come from Hank Dennis's savings account.

What held Joe Fogarty's attention was not the people going into the store or coming out, it was that top buggy with the red wheels. It was parked squarely in front of the emporium.

Several idlers were standing in overhang shade out front admiring the elegant rig and its team of matched chestnut sorrels. When the marshal came along, a beanpole of a man chewing a straw said, "It's one of them new Studebakers, Marshal. Got a little brass plate on the back of the bed that says so. Look at them little steel springs stacked one atop the other, each one shorter'n the one under it. How much do you expect a buggy like that'd cost a man?''

Joe had no idea. He admired the rig, but he admired the matched sorrels more. He had his back to the doorway of the store when a voice he knew belonged to Hank Dennis said, "That's him. The big man yonder.''

Joe turned. Hank was going back into his store leaving a redheaded woman standing there. She had eyes as blue as cornflowers. Joe touched his hat brim while groping for words. Whoever she was, she had to be the most handsome female he had ever seen. "Joe Fogarty, ma'am,'' he said.

The handsome woman smiled. "I'm new to the country, Marshal. I've been trying to find someone who can give me some directions.''

Joe knew the idlers were watching him, forgetting momentarily about the Studebaker buggy. He said, "Be glad to help. I was just going to the cafe for coffee. I'd be pleased if you'd let me buy you a cup.''

The handsome woman had flesh the color of new cream. She was fairly tall for a woman, about five feet five or six inches, with every bit of it fleshed out in perfect proportion. She said, "Will the horses be all right?''

The beanpole chewing a straw drawled an answer to her question. "Yes'm. I'd be glad to keep an eye on 'em for you.''

The handsome woman said, "Thank you,'' and walked southward with Town Marshal Fogarty. Behind them the idlers watched for a while, until Fogarty and the redheaded woman entered the cafe. Then the beanpole spat out his straw, glanced at his expressionless companions, and burst out laughing. Eventually, he said, "I've known the marshal four years, seen him clean out

Morton's saloon of a Saturday night with his hands; I never seen but maybe one or two men in my whole life that got the sick-calf look on their faces like he had."

A short, heavy man nodded while wiping his eyes from laughing so hard. As he returned his attention to the parked hitch and buggy, he said, "Mr. Fogarty could do a lot worse. I'd guess them chestnut sorrels to be worth seventy-five dollars each. And he'd get the buggy thrown in."

The laughter broke out again as the idlers had their attention diverted by the arrival at the north end of town of the midday stage from up north. This daily event was always a source of interest. All but the thin man who had said he'd watch the redheaded lady's rig went shuffling up to take positions in overhang shade out front of the abstract office, where they could watch passengers climb out of the coach in the corralyard and walk back to the plank walk. Strangers were examined and categorized as they appeared past the corralyard gates.

Usually, they made a beeline for either the rooming house or the cafe. Today, two traveling drummers in matching britches and coats broke the pattern by leaving the other passengers and heading directly for Morton's saloon.

The other passengers walked toward the rooming house. No one seemed interested in the cafe at the moment, which was just as well. The cafe did very little business this time of the morning, which satisfied Marshal Fogarty as he tipped back his hat, ordered two coffees, and smiled as the handsome woman said, "It's a pretty town, Marshal. Except for the trees lining Main Street, it would be just another small town, wouldn't it?"

Joe nodded. "And the folks are friendly too, ma'am." He waited until the coffee had been served and the cafeman had departed after making a furtively admiring study of Joe's companion. "Sort of hot this time of year."

She tasted the coffee and put the cup down. "It's hot most places this time of year, Marshal. Where I come from it's hot every summer."

Joe nodded. "Directly now the nights'll start cooling off." Joe warmed to this discussion. "In the northward mountains it's ten, maybe fifteen degrees cooler." He looked at her. "There's some beautiful country up there. A few lakes of the bluest water you ever saw. Lots of trout in 'em."

She smiled at him. "You like it very much. I hope I learn to."

He continued to watch as she lifted the coffee cup again. There was no wedding ring. He straightened forward. "You will. Everyone does if they stay here very long."

An older man with gingery hair walked in, looked startled at what he saw sitting at the counter next to the marshal, nodded curtly to Fogarty, and went to the lower end of the counter.

Joe leaned a little. "That's Mr. McGregor. He's got the gun shop in town."

The handsome woman glanced at James, who was studying his hands atop the counter as the cafeman came along and looked up to say, "Java an' a piece of pie if you got it."

The cafeman's gaze whipped to the handsome woman as he went past. Over at the pie table he sighed and rolled his eyes.

Fogarty had finished his coffee. The woman had not and evidently was not going to. Joe thought that perhaps where she came from they didn't drink coffee that was made fresh just once a week, otherwise; if it got weak along toward the middle of the week, folks threw in another fistful of ground beans.

She said, "Marshal, I'm looking for a particular ranch."

Joe nodded. "Yes'm. I know every outfit for fifty miles in all directions." He gazed at her flawless profile. "Some are quite a ways out. Most of them are, in fact, and it's a little late in the day to start out. I'd be happy to walk you down to the rooming house. You could strike out early in the morning."

The very blue eyes were warmly appreciative. "That's very kind of you, but according to the letter I have, the place I'm looking for isn't very far from Sheridan." She rummaged in a handbag in her lap.

James McGregor got his pie and coffee, cleared his throat, and when Fogarty turned, the gunsmith looked skyward and sighed. Joe reddened but otherwise ignored the gunsmith.

The handsome woman unfolded a slip of white paper, studied it for a moment, then said, "I'm looking for the Holbert place."

For three seconds there was not a sound in the cafe. Even roadway noises seemed muted. McGregor, with a forkful of pie midway to his mouth, was staring at the handsome woman as though mesmerized.

She leaned to brush shoulders with Joe Fogarty as she held the letter where he could see it. "It's from my brother. He bought a ranch west of here last spring after selling out back home in Texas." The blue eyes swept up to Joe's face. "Jed Holbert?"

Fogarty's lips barely moved. "Yes'm. We've met. He was in town until a couple of hours ago."

She was putting the letter back into her purse as she

asked how far the ranch was from town and in which direction. Joe pushed up to his feet, counted out some silver, and left it atop the counter. He shot a glance toward the lower end of the cafe, but McGregor was concentrating on his coffee and pie so their eyes did not meet.

Fogarty said nothing as he walked the handsome woman back up to her rig, handed her up into it, and showed her a sad smile. "Due west, ma'am. About ten miles. You can't miss it. The country's flat out there. Your brother's place will be the only set of buildings you'll see."

She held out a warm hand. When he took it she squeezed gently. "Thank you for the coffee, Marshal. You've been very kind and helpful, and I think you are right; the folks in Sheridan country are friendly."

He stepped ahead, lifted the tether weight, unhooked its halter snap from the near-side sorrel's bit, and placed the weight in the rig. She evened up the lines, shot him a beautiful smile, and straightened her matched sorrels to make a wide sashay heading for the lower end of town, where wagon ruts led westerly.

Joe reset his hat. Behind him the beanpole had another straw to chew on. He, too, watched the rig out of sight, then he strolled up to join his friends in the shade out in front of the abstract office.

Joe was still standing there watching a thin plume of feathery dust rising over beyond town where the handsome woman was heading west. He did not see McGregor approaching.

Because he was a prudent man at times, the gunsmith hiked on past and stepped down into the roadway up by the emporium, heading on a diagonal course toward the harness shop. When he walked in up there he rolled his eyes and said, "Hugh, that feller named Holbert . . ."

"Yeah. What about him?"

"He's got the prettiest woman for a sister you ever saw. She left Joe Fogarty standin' down in front of the cafe like he'd taken root."

Pepperdine was still sewing sheep pelt on that pigeon-wing saddle skirt. "Did Joe know who she was?"

"She told him, asked how to get out to her brother's ranch. You should have seen the marshal's face. He looked worse than you did down there in the Howe's barn after the shooting stopped."

Hugh leaned to aim for his sandbox, sprayed amber, and shook his head. "And he lost a hundred and fifty dollars too." Pepperdine climbed off the sewing horse, dug beneath his counter, set up the little sticky glasses and a bottle, and poured solemnly. "We ought to drink to Joe Fogarty who is sometimes lucky and sometimes unlucky. When he's unlucky, he's unlucky all over."

They raised their glasses.

One of the passengers off the midday stage walked in. He was a rangy-built man who favored black. There was a Colt with a carved handle visible beneath his coat when he moved. He'd just come from the saloon, where they had told him he might look in at the harness works for the town marshal before he went on down the same side of the road to the jailhouse.

He said he was a deputy marshal from Denver; his name was Sam Wells. He said all this after Hugh told him Joe Fogarty had not been in his shop since much earlier.

Sam Wells was an impressive, lean, tall, hawk-faced man with very dark hair and eyes. He looked to be in his forties. McGregor and Pepperdine watched him with more curiosity than interest, particularly since he had not departed after being told the person he was looking for was not there.

Wells gazed steadily at the older men and finally said, "They also told me over at the saloon about you gents and Mr. Fogarty running down Hy Simpson and his crew."

Hugh's face cleared. "You're looking for Simpson?"

"*Was* looking for him. He's dead, isn't he?"

"Yes, sir. Him an' all but a couple of his friends. They are down at the jailhouse."

Sam Wells's very dark eyes twinkled faintly. "You gents don't look like gunfighters," he said.

McGregor answered shortly. "We aren't. Where we cornered Simpson there was no call for fast drawin' or a lot of accurate shooting. It was more like a battle."

Wells's expression did not change. "Thanks, gents. I'd better go hunt up Marshal Fogarty."

They watched him turn southward on the plank walk. Hugh refilled the little glasses. "Now, there's a man I wouldn't want to steal horses from," he said, lifting his little glass. "This evening we could hunt up Joe and find out what Mr. Wells came down here for. Most likely it'll have to do with the bounty money. Joe'll have to prove they're dead, and from the personal things he brought back, that shouldn't be too hard."

McGregor dropped down his whiskey, slapped the countertop, and blew out a fiery breath. As he turned to leave he said, "I hope that bounty money does me more good than your whiskey does."

Hugh reared back. "What's wrong with my whiskey?"

"Tastes like it's got flour in it instead of malt."

"Why, you old ingrate, that's special whiskey all the way from Kansas."

McGregor reached the plank walk without looking back or speaking. He stepped down into the dust in the direction of his shop without knowing that Hugh glared after him and said, "Flour! Damned old oatmeal carcass!"

ABOUT THE AUTHOR

Lauran Paine lives in Greenview, California. He is an accomplished western writer who has published dozens of books under various pseudonyms and his own name. THE GUNS OF SUMMER is the first in the series of the forthcoming Sheridan Township Westerns.